THE
MISSING
PIECE

KIERSTEN MODGLIN

To my husband, Michael, for being my high school love story.
To my sisters, Kaitie, Kortnee, and Kyleigh, for filling my
childhood with love, laughter, and strange Halloween costumes.
I love you all!

CHAPTER ONE

Someone once told me that eventually time takes away everything you have—everyone you love, your dreams, your memories, your fears. It takes everything you've ever had, and you never notice until it's gone. The same person told me that though time is known to heal, time is actually cruel. Despite every single thing time steals from you, it will never take one thing away. No matter how many nights you spend awake, how many meals you miss, or how many stares you try not to notice; time is just time, and no matter how much time passes, it will never let you forget the truth.

My room is painted a sickly pastel pink. For the record, I hate pink with every fiber of my being. My mom picked out the color years ago, and for whatever reason, it stuck.

My mom died when I was fifteen, and she was replaced by a fake smile on a silent face. My entire world fell apart when I was fifteen. I remember a time when every morning was filled with the smell of bacon cooking and the sound of my mother's laughter. Dad could always be found close by reading a newspaper with a charming smile on his face and a steaming cup of coffee in front of him. I don't know the last time any of us looked at a newspaper. They're off-limits now.

My alarm clock rang out, but it was pointless. I had been awake since 4:04, just like always. I looked around my dark room, heaving a sigh. I had been boarded into the same room my whole life. It changed as I did, going from posters of *The Little Mermaid* and *Barney*, to kiss-worthy pictures of Chad Michael Murray and NSYNC, and most recently, to nothing—to blankness, the empti-ness I felt inside.

I could describe everything in my room by memory. Beside my bed sat a small desk with my ringing alarm clock and a book that I should have read months ago for a class I couldn't pretend to care about. Although I could see only a vague outline, I knew that the wall I was facing contained the only thing hanging up in my now bare room. It was a drawing of me, a simple pencil sketch that had faded with age, but it made me look more beautiful than the mirror ever could. Years ago, when I started high school, I had been surprised to find it taped to my locker. It was perfect, beautiful. I had asked around, trying to find a clue to point me to the artist, but no one claimed it. Eventually, I had just given up. It had never really mattered to me who had drawn it, perhaps a crush too shy to come out, maybe a cheerleader thinking it would be funny to draw my nose a little bigger than it was in real-ity. In the end, I'd kept it, deciding to display it proudly on my wall like a trophy. I chose to believe it was a good thing, a sign that somewhere out there, I had a friend.

Coming back to reality, I let out a groan, pressing my fingers onto the plastic of the clock to halt the sound. I brushed my hair from my eyes, pulling the string of my lamp and allowing it to illuminate my room. Rubbing sleep from my eyes, I pulled the blanket off of my legs, welcoming the cool air. Getting up was the easy part. Facing the day was where it got hard.

CHAPTER TWO

S *tep, step, grab door handle, pull door handle, smile, walk.* I told myself how to move and what to do, keeping my mind focused on only that. These days, it was so hard to concentrate on anything for too long.

I entered the school building with my head down, walking toward the corner near the back of the lobby I was so familiar with. My corner. My safe spot. I passed dozens of students, each lost in their own world, no one making eye contact with me. That was okay. I liked it that way.

As I neared my corner, I stopped. There was something unfamiliar waiting for me. He wore a blue button-up shirt: simple, safe. His hair was blond, reminding me of the inside of a banana. It swept over his eyes carefully. His eyes met mine; they were brown—warm, calm. He was saying something. He was staring at me.

"I'm Brayden," he said, gazing up at me with a half-smile on his face. He asked if he was in my spot.

Yes, you are. Move. "Uh, no. You're okay," I heard myself answer. *Good job. Now smile back.*

I turned quickly to walk away, before he could ask me anything else. My heart pounded in my chest, telling me to get away. *Faster. Faster.*

"Where are you going?" I heard him call out from behind me.

I kept walking, afraid to answer, afraid to turn around. The hairs on back of my neck stood up. Nothing felt right. I heard his shoes squeak on the floor as he stood up. I heard him rushing to keep up with me.

I jumped as he touched my back gently, trying to make me stop. He pulled away. "Look, I'm sorry if I took your spot or your corner or whatever. I can totally go somewhere else, honest. It's not a big deal."

I stopped walking, turning to face him. "It's fine. Seriously. It's not like my name is on the corner or something." I looked hopefully toward the corner, feeling his eyes resting on me anxiously. I avoided his gaze, trying desperately to slow my pounding heart. It was pathetic, really, how nervous I was. I took a deep breath. *Good girl. Stay calm.*

He smiled. "Go ahead." He gestured toward the corner. "I have to go find my locker, anyway."

I nodded, looking away and hoping he would leave. *Am I supposed to say 'thank you' now?* After a few awkward seconds, I turned and walked shyly toward the corner, pressing my back into the cool wall as I slid down. I closed my eyes, feeling my heart rate finally slow down. I reached into my purse, pulling out a book and flipping it open, silencing my racing thoughts. No sooner had I finally begun to read, than a pair of legs slid down beside me. The smell of his cologne burned my nose. It was peppery. I glanced up, hoping that an annoyed look radiated from my face.

"Hey." He smiled at me nonchalantly.

I nodded. "I thought you were going to go find your locker?"

"Oh yeah, I totally forgot that I'd already found it. My bad." His eyes focused on mine with a vice-like grip. The corners of his mouth turned up coyly.

I looked away, willing him to shut up. What was his problem? Why couldn't he just leave me alone? What had I done to deserve this?

"Am I bothering you or something?"

I didn't bother to look his way, instead turning the page pointedly. "No."

"Cool. So, what's your name?"

Silence. *Take the hint, boy, please.*

"You do have a name, don't you?" It was like the boy had never even heard of a hint.

I slammed my book closed, raising my eyebrows to look his way. "Yes, I do have a name. I'm Jaicey."

"Jaicey, huh? Well, it's very nice to meet you, Jaicey. I'm Brayden."

"Yeah. You said that already." I didn't smile.

"Right." He smiled. His smile was nice, warm in a way that would've had other girls blushing. *Other girls. Normal girls. Girls not like me.*

I looked back down, ignoring the pressure of his eyes on my face, and tried to focus on the book I was attempting to read. I refused to let my heart speed up again. *You're fine*, I told myself. *You're safe*. Finally, he turned away, pulling out a book of his own and beginning to read as well. I sat as the minutes passed, flipping aimlessly through a book I wasn't truly reading. Instead, I just skimmed the pages, waiting for the bell to ring. I couldn't focus on anything but him. He was entirely too close to me. It was distracting, and I *don't* mean that in a good way. I could feel the heat of his skin only inches from mine. I could hear him breathing, see each page as it turned in his hand. It gave me chills. Finally, I was given relief. As the bell sounded, I all but jumped up, racing away from him and refusing to look back.

CHAPTER THREE

Some things never change. Take school, for instance. No matter where you go, what grade you're in, or who you are, you'll always find the same kids. There are the kids who everyone secretly wants to be, the ones who are members of the country club, whose fathers could buy them a whole city if they wanted to; the people with their designer clothes, beautiful faces and perfect lives. There are the people who honestly don't care about anything; the ones who are comfortable with themselves, usually for extremely unobvious reasons. There are the kids who can quote whole books, who can answer any question correctly. And then, there are the kids who just fade into the background, the kids who you'll look back at in your yearbook in five years and not remember them at all.

As I walked down the hall toward first hour, I prayed to be forgotten. I held my breath, tucking my chin into my chest and heading quickly toward my classroom, focusing on my feet. Then I heard it.

"Jaicey." *Keep walking,* I willed myself. Maybe I had

heard wrong, but the voice was unmistakable. I felt her perfectly moisturized hands grasp my arm, her fingers wrapping around my wrist like talons. "Jaice, hey. It's me," she said again. I was stuck; there was no way out.

I looked up, feigning surprise. *Smile.* "Oh, hey, Mallory. I didn't see you."

"Oh my god, Jaicey, I can't believe it. I heard you were back. Everyone will be so glad. It's so good to finally see you. We've missed you so much. How've you been?" If it was possible, her teeth had gotten even whiter since I'd been gone.

Horrible. Terrible. Leave me alone. "Fine. You?"

"Oh, I'm amazing." She waved me off. "If you hadn't heard the rumors already, Tyler asked me to prom. It happened last week. He went all out with balloons and flowers. I wish you could've been there to see it," she exclaimed, as if that weren't already a given. Homecoming Queen and Quarterback—could she be more cliché? I put on my best smile, my gaze drifting away from her face as I tried not to roll my eyes.

"Oh, congratulations. I hope you have fun." What I really hoped was that I was doing a good job of looking like I cared.

"Aww, thank you. I think we will." She smiled at me brightly. "Hey, you know, I've heard Derek is still looking for a date. I don't know if he knew what to do about prom...after everything. You know, I wonder if he even knows you're back yet. I haven't seen much of him lately, honestly. He's been so out of it. Not that I blame him, you know..." She trailed off. Then, seeming to remember what she was talking about, she clasped her hands in front of her chest. "Oh, he'll be so happy to see you, and of course, I'm sure he'd love to go with you. What do you say? Oh, look at me. Here I go, rambling. I should let him actually ask you first, right? You know how I get…always one step ahead."

Smile. I paused. *Was she actually asking me out for someone else? The poor guy deserved better.* "You know what, Mallory? I can't go. I actually already had plans for that night. Sucks. I wish I'd known sooner," came the automatic response.

She pursed her lips. "Jaicey, come on, girl. We miss you. You know we'd all love to hang out with you again. All of us. We've all called dozens of times, even come by to visit you. They said you just needed space. We understood, but we're your friends. We just wanted to see you."

"I'm sorry. Some other time, maybe. I really have to get to class. I can't be late already." I smiled and hurried off before she could get in another word. The popular kids at my school think it's funny to pretend to be nice to those of us who aren't like them. Pretty, popular, rich. We all know they make fun of us behind our backs. I, unlike so many others, never fall for their games. I scowled as I heard her voice ringing in my head. *We miss you!* How can you miss something you never had?

STARES. I felt them. I looked around, meeting Wyatt Grey's eyes. He smiled. His gaze fell to my neck. I leaned my head over, flashing him a dirty look. He looked away quickly, but not before Mr. Putt noticed what happened.

He gave Wyatt a warning look, and then continued on with his discussion on World War II.

I offered Mr. Putt a thankful grin, but he didn't acknowledge me. Not that I cared. Add him to the long list of people who don't acknowledge me. Mr. Putt was new at our school, starting only last year. He was friendly enough, but he still felt like a placeholder. Our old teacher, Mr. Brown, had retired the year before, much to our dismay. Mr. Brown was my favorite teacher and I missed him dearly. *Not much longer,* I remind myself, because I'm counting down the days until I don't have to return to this place ever again. *Lucky Mr. Brown.*

CHAPTER FOUR

After school that day, I walked out toward the buses and I heard yet another familiar voice. "Oh my god! Well, look who we have here. If it isn't Miss-Too-Cool-For-School herself, gracing us all with her presence. Where have you been?"

I turned, knowing that no matter how bad I wanted to, I wouldn't be able to keep walking. Derek was a lot closer than I had expected. His blue eyes burned into mine, extinguishing the breath in my lungs immediately, just like they always had. I reminded myself that this was normal. He was every girl's crush and *so* out of my league. Still, I couldn't help but appreciate the way his brown hair curled around his ears, his perfect, football-playing build, and his beautiful, white smile. My heart bellowed in my chest and I felt blood rush to my cheeks.

"Hey, Derek. How are you?" I mumbled, immediately kicking myself for not having something cute or witty to say.

"Better now. It's so good to see you. I've been hoping

you'd be back soon. No one really knew what to expect. But hey, you know what's coming up, right? What do you say to a few Friday nights from now: you, me, some spiked punch, and a full night of dancing?"

"I don't dance, Derek." My response was immediate. *Could he actually be serious?*

"What are you talking about? You love dancing." He frowned, pulling my hands away from my sides as if we were going to start dancing right then.

"I do not. How would you even know what I love?" I tried to downplay the unexpected anger in my voice.

"Come on, Jaice, please don't be like that. You have to go with me. It's our Senior Prom. You just have to. Please? Pretty, pretty please?" He dropped my hands, touching my face, his skin burning mine.

Flinch. I swallowed loudly, breaking eye contact as embarrassment engulfed me. "It's okay, really. You'll have more fun with someone else. I have a lot going on that night. I'm sorry."

"I want to go with you, though," he insisted. His stare made me feel dizzy. He leaned in toward me, until his breath hit my cheek. I stared into his eyes, the kind of eyes that you could get lost in. For just a moment, I forgot where I was, forgot what I knew. Everything faded away and all I could see what his face, his beautiful face. Then, without warning, he did it. He glanced toward my neck— just for a split second—but I'd seen it and my moment was over. The world came back to me.

I pulled his hand down from my face. "I don't think so. Maybe another time, okay?" Without giving him a chance to answer, I walked away. My face burned from awkwardness, my feet carrying me away without my own volition. I just wanted to get away from him, from this place. I heard him calling my name but I couldn't look back. I wouldn't.

I was almost to the bus stop when I heard a voice behind me. "Boyfriend?" This was a voice I didn't immediately recognize.

I turned abruptly. "Huh?" There he was—a face I had nearly forgotten. I paused, unsure of what to say. "Oh, you're Brayden, right?"

He was standing next to a tiny, blue car, grinning broadly at me. His smile was far from perfect and his hair was standing up in random places, but I could tell he didn't care. I took a moment to look him over properly, a chance I hadn't been given this morning. His face was confident. He had a stance that made him look strong, even though his build was slightly smaller than most guys our age. He laughed, obviously enjoying my stares. I looked down quickly. "Yeah," he said, "you remembered. Good to hear. You seemed kind of out of it when we met. I didn't know if you'd even recognize me."

I let a tiny smile creep onto my lips. "Yeah, believe it or not, I actually get that a lot. Sorry—did you say something to me?"

He gestured to behind me, where I was sure Derek would still be talking to his friends. "I asked if that was your boyfriend."

"*Derek?*" I shrieked, probably too quickly. "Oh, no. No. He's just Derek." I let out a laugh that seemed a little crazy.

He smiled again; I noticed a dimple on his left cheek

that I hadn't seen before. He was cute in a quirky way, far opposite of Derek. "So, where's your car?"

"Oh, I, um, I don't have a car," I admitted.

"Oh." He paused. "Well, get in, then. Do you need a ride home? I don't mind."

"No. I take the bus." I took a step backward, pointing to the stop, and gasped. The buses were gone. I had never even noticed them pulling away.

"Aren't you, like, a senior? And you're still taking the bus?" He snickered. "How old are you? Are you one of those freaky smart kids who skipped a grade or something?"

"I'm almost eighteen," I snipped. "I'm old enough to drive and I'm in the right grade, *thank you very much.* I just don't want to drive."

"You're kidding." He looked at me as if I'd said I wanted to live in the wilderness for the rest of my life and live on bugs and wild animals.

"No, I'm not kidding at all," I insisted.

"What do you mean you *don't want* to drive? Of course you want to drive. Everyone wants to drive."

"Not me. I'm going to live in the city so I'll never need to learn to drive. I'll probably just take cabs everywhere or something. If I live in New York, I can take the subway. There are tons of people who don't drive. It isn't the end of the world," I told him heatedly.

"Oh, so in other words, you're scared." He frowned, teasing me tirelessly.

"I'm not scared," I said defensively, "but I do have to go. I'll be really late if I don't leave soon."

"You can't be serious. You're going to walk? Home? No

way. Seriously, no. Get in. It's no big deal. I can't let you walk home." He pointed toward his car.

"I'm not walking home. My mom works a block away. I could use the exercise, anyway. I'll be fine." To be nice, I threw in, "Thanks, though." I turned to walk away, believing for a second I had gotten away, as I heard his engine rev up. Then came his voice again as his car pulled up beside me, window rolled down. "Hey, so, you never told me why you said no?"

"Said no to what?" I asked, not slowing my pace.

"To Drake when he asked you to prom."

I glanced at him, a curious look filling my face. How in the world had he known Derek had asked me to prom?

"Sorry, I overheard." He shrugged, answering the question I hadn't asked.

I looked straight ahead again, refusing to look his way. "His name's Derek, not Drake."

"Okay, Derek, then. Why'd you say no to *Derek*?" He emphasized his name.

I stopped walking, one hand on my hip, the other held up to block the sun from my eyes. "Because I didn't want to go."

"Of course you did," he said simply, his head cocked to the side.

"Why do you keep telling me what I want to do?"

"Because you want to go to prom."

"How would you know?"

"Well...because everyone wants to go to prom," he replied.

"Not me," I said indignantly.

16

"That's not possible. And it's not a reason. You can't say no for no reason. It's just weird."

"Well, that's the only reason I have. Sorry." I took a deep breath, turning to walk away once more.

"No," he said.

I stopped again, staring at him in disbelief. "No? What do you mean?"

"*No*. I reject your answer and request another, kind lady." He donned a fake British accent and tipped his head at the end for good measure.

"Why can't I decide I don't want to go to prom? People *don't* go to prom all the time."

"Because they aren't asked. Or because they have something else going on, sure. But not because they just don't want to go. That's just…weird."

"Well, maybe I'm weird." I crossed my arms.

"You aren't."

I furrowed my brow at him.

"You just aren't," he said, to answer my unspoken question again.

"You obviously don't know me, Brayden." I shook my head at him.

"I'm trying to fix that, *Jaicey*." He said my name back to me, that cocky smile still plastered on his face.

"Trust me, you shouldn't bother wasting your time. Neither should Derek. Which, for the record, is why I said no."

"Why?"

He was stubborn, I'd give him that.

"Because I'm just…boring. I'd be a boring date. He'd

have an awful, boring time. Besides that, I do actually have other plans," I lied.

"Other plans on prom night? Yeah, right. What could be more important than hanging out with your friends?"

"I don't have friends." The seriousness in my tone caused my voice to quiver.

He stopped the car abruptly, leaning over in his seat and extending his hand through the window. "Hi, I'm Brayden. I'm new here. Would you care to be my friend?"

I stared at him in disbelief. Even though he was a good foot away from me, I had flinched when he moved his hand toward me. The strange look on his face told me it hadn't gone unnoticed.

"Sorry, but no," I said simply, humiliation filling me. I looked down at the pavement, staring at my scuffed-up sneakers.

"Why not?" he asked, unmoving, his hand still outstretched.

"I told you. I don't have friends. I don't want friends," I called behind me as I began to walk again.

"Everyone needs friends, Jaicey. Didn't you watch *Barney* growing up? Come on now, that's *Barney* 101."

I ignored his joke with single-minded determination. "Not me, I don't believe in friendship. Friends are just enemies who know all your biggest secrets and are waiting for a chance to use them against you."

He started the car again. He wasn't giving up. "Boy, you sure are cynical."

"I'm not cynical. I'm honest and I'm realistic and I don't live in some happy bubble believing that the world is full of goodness and love and if you are just kind to your neighbor everything will work out. That's all just crap; there's too much bad in the world. Friends don't fix that. More people should realize that."

"All right." He sighed, his voice sounding defeated. "Whatever you say. I'll see you tomorrow." He laughed again, turning up his music and speeding away.

CHAPTER FIVE

"How was school, Jaice?" My mom's voice echoed through the quiet kitchen.

I nodded, not really looking her direction. "It was fine, Mom."

"I talked to Rebecca Anderson this afternoon. She asked about you. Did you see Derek at school today?"

I half-smiled. "Yeah, I did. Just for a second after school ended."

"Did you get to talk to him?"

"No. Not really. Why?"

"Oh, I was just wondering," Mom answered. I took another bite of my food. "Did he ask you to prom?" Mom *wondered* some more, bottled excitement in her voice.

"No, he just said hello," I lied. It wasn't worth it to tell her the truth. She'd only be disappointed.

"Oh. Well, that's okay. You know what? I wish you would go hang out with friends this week. I know how much you must miss them. I think it'd be really good for you to get out. I'm sure everyone would love to see you.

Rebecca said the kids have been just dying for you to come back."

I pushed my plate of barely-touched food away from me. My mother's naïveté hurt me. She knew they didn't want to see me. Why would they? She just couldn't admit that her child wasn't part of the *in* crowd. It killed her that I wasn't the cheerleader she'd been in high school. I'd never be who she wanted me to be. Rather than fight, I simply shrugged. "Maybe next week, Mom. I've got tons of homework to catch up on."

"But, Jaice—"

My dad sighed, holding his hand up to stop my mom. "Okay, baby, that's fine. Let us know if you need any help."

I stood up, leaving the conversation unfinished, just as I did every night. I looked back at my parents; my mom eating her food, staring blankly into space, and my father avoiding eye contact with us both. This was what my family had become. Shortly after turning fifteen, I entered a no-parent household.

THE NEXT DAY AT SCHOOL, I was met at the door by Alyssa Fuller, one of Mallory's friends. *Smile,* I willed myself. Her black hair bounced above her shoulders as she ran toward me, her skin radiating a tan that looked as though she must've just come from vacation.

"Jaicey! Girl! What the *heck* is up? I heard you're going to prom with Derek? Congrats! I'm so excited for you."

Alyssa had always had an ear for drama. "Uh, no, he, uh, he asked me. But I'm visiting family that weekend, so

I had to say no." I put on my best pretend-to-be-sad face.

She put her arm around me. "Oh, honey. That's too bad." Without missing a beat, she went on. "So, did you hear they opened up a new skating rink across town? Boneheads or something like that...I can't remember the name. Anyway, everybody's going to check it out soon. You have to come!"

I smiled and ducked out of her embrace quickly, a cloud of her perfume engulfing me. "Yeah, definitely. I mean, maybe. I'll let you know. Anyway, I'm sorry I can't talk longer but I've got to get to my locker. I'm always late for first period. We'll talk later." *Smile.*

She waved happily as I scrambled from her grasp. "Okay, sure. Well, call me! We have to catch up!" She kept talking, even as I walked away. I kept walking, pretending not to hear a word.

I was surprised to see Brayden sitting quietly in the corner, reading, just as he had been the day before. He turned the page of his book, never looking up at me. Before he could see me, I began to walk down the hallway. I would have to find a new hiding spot. After about five steps, I heard his voice behind me. "You know...I don't bite. I'd be willing to swear to that in a court of law."

I turned on my heel, staring at him oddly. He just smiled and looked back down at his book, daring me to sit next to him. Something came over me, a braveness I hadn't known before, and I smiled back. *Dare accepted.*

CHAPTER SIX

The next week, my room was unnaturally cold when I got home. I slipped on my sweatpants and a big T-shirt, then jumped into bed. I reached over and turned my phone on silent. I didn't want to be bothered. Honestly, it wasn't like anyone would call, but the satisfaction that came with knowing that they couldn't made me feel safe.

I closed my eyes, rolled over, and entered my bubble. I didn't want to think. I just wanted to drift off to sleep. I welcomed sleep like an old friend. My dreams, much like the rest of my life, were empty and dark. In both worlds, I found myself alone. When I was young, I could never remember my dreams. Now, the familiar loneliness in them found me immediately upon waking.

I wasn't sure how long I'd been asleep when a scream tore me from my slumber. It had me up out of bed faster than I thought possible. I tossed my covers aside quickly, darting from the room. It was loud, blaring and roaring in my sleep-coated mind. It penetrated my thoughts until I could focus on nothing else. The scream was mesmerizing. It made my head spin and I could feel cool tears gathering in my eyes. *Calm down*, I willed myself, but it was all so loud. Finally, relief came in the form of darkness as I tumbled to the floor.

THE LIGHT BURNED my opening eyes, and, for a split second, I thought maybe it had all been a dream. I realized quickly, however, that the screaming in my head could still be heard and it was not actually inside my head but coming from somewhere in the house. It had turned into more of a moan now. Somewhere in the distance, I could hear voices. The scream was coming from so far away, I doubted I could ever make it in time. Something was in my house, invading my safety. I wanted it to go away. I stood up and instinctively grabbed my head. It felt so heavy.

"*Stop screaming!*" I yelled. "*Stop it! Stop it, please!*" I bellowed out a scream of my own. It had to stop. The screaming stopped, as if on command. Then, after a brief pause, I heard, "Jaicey? Jaicey…please help."

I forced myself to stand up, though my legs still felt like jelly. I walked in a dreamlike state, listening carefully for her muffled cries. "Mom?" I called out. I followed the cries and found myself in her bedroom. "Momma?" When I finally saw her, fear gripped my stomach and my knees buckled. I fell to the floor again.

Crouched down so close to the floor I could smell the carpet, I crawled up to her, forcing my body to move. She was lying face down on a crumpled pile of clothes. I said her name once more, approaching her slowly. I grabbed her arm apprehensively, lightly shaking her, willing her to tell me what was happening. "What's wrong?" I watched her body shake with sobs. Finally, she lifted her head, meeting my eyes.

"Call nine-one-one, Jaicey. Please. Call nine-one-one." I looked down at her lap, where my father's head lay. His eyes were wide open, his face solid as stone. There was a string of vomit hanging off his chin, leading to a puddle in the floor.

"Dad?" I asked, my voice shaking. He didn't look at me. "What's wrong with him?" I begged my mother.

She grabbed my arm, squeezing it tightly. "Jaicey, now! *Go!*"

Her fingers dug into my skin, her grip hurting me. Everything in my body grew cold. I jerked away from her grasp, her nails leaving trails of blood behind. Her face filled with fear, knowing what she'd done. I scrambled backward, trying to get away as fast as possible. "*Don't touch me!*" I screamed at her, my voice so feral and animal-like I didn't recognize it. "Don't you ever touch me!"

I tripped twice while running out of the room, though I couldn't stop. I had to find safety. I couldn't bring myself to look back at my mother's sobbing face, but I could hear her crying out to me. It wasn't until I was behind my locked door that my breathing slowed and my heart rate calmed. Five minutes later, once I could catch my breath, I called 911.

CHAPTER SEVEN

When I was a little girl, my dad used to bounce me on his knee and sing to me whenever I was afraid. It quickly became our little ritual. I remember the day it started.

It was the night before I started kindergarten, and I was worried about starting school, worried about making friends. I tried to pretend that I wasn't scared, but my parents knew better. After dinner, Mom told me to get my pajamas on. I did. When I came back to the living room to say goodnight, my dad scooped me over his shoulder and sat me down on his knee. Then he bounced his knee, singing a song loudly—off-key and out of tune— but I didn't care. It felt like that moment lasted forever. I remember how hard we laughed. I remember my cheeks burning from the excitement and adrenaline. When it was over, he hugged me close and whispered, "You have scared eyes. Don't be scared, Jaice. Daddy's not going to let anything hurt you." It was almost instantaneous, the relief that washed over me. Just like that, I wasn't afraid anymore. Without ever speaking of it, this little ceremony became ours. We did it every year, before my first day of school. Eventually, I claimed that I was too big to sit in his lap anymore and he understood, but he still offered every single year.

———

WHEN WE ARRIVED at the hospital Mom was still panicked, shouting orders at everyone in sight. I was in shock, ignoring every order she shouted, and my dad was unconscious. *Lucky him.* The doctors took him into a room and ordered me and Mom out. We must have sat there for hours, waiting and watching, standing hopefully as each doctor strode past us. We had no idea what to do with the silence of the hallway, so eventually, sleep found me and I graciously welcomed it.

CHAPTER EIGHT

A brain tumor.

No, correction, a *malignant brain tumor.* An inoperable, malignant brain tumor. That's what the doctor had called it. That's what was growing inside of my dad. As we walked into the hospital room, I saw that Dad was sitting up in bed, but he still looked exhausted. He smiled at me, though I couldn't bring myself to smile back. He had a tumor. A brain tumor, stage two. *It was a tumor.* I tried to run it through my head over and over until it made sense. So far, it hadn't worked.

My mom was talking to the doctor with a solemn, serious face. Business all the time—that was my mom. She had never been the type to show emotion or let any situation affect her. She was a closed door. A locked window no one could break through. Of that, I can say I learned from the very best.

"Imagine talking to someone telling you to go left while pointing right," the doctor was explaining. "That's what a tumor does. It mixes up all the signals. Your husband's brain is telling his body to do one thing, but the tumor says the other. As the tumor grows, it's likely that everything in his body will see an adverse effect."

My mother was nodding, her lips pressed into a thin line, as if he were telling her that he liked the color red.

"Of course, all the symptoms aren't expected anytime soon. It looks like he had a mild seizure and hit his head. Fortunately, there was no swelling. Nothing too serious yet. We're going to need to go ahead and schedule his first few rounds of chemo and radiation, obviously. I'll get you with my nurse to see what sort of schedule we can start him out on."

My mother followed him into the hallway, and I walked up to my dad's bed cautiously, my gaze glued to the floor. I pulled myself up beside him so that I could touch him, but I couldn't meet his eyes. We were quiet for a while, both of us staring off into space. Every part of me ached. This wasn't fair.

"Well, looks like I gave you all quite a scare," my dad said finally, breaking the ice.

I smiled halfheartedly. "Yeah."

He touched my hand. I tried to resist flinching, but it happened anyway. He moved it back without saying a word, a confirmation that I was still as broken as before. I couldn't change.

I tried to fill the quiet. "So, how do you feel? Do you feel differently? Does anything hurt?"

"I'm okay. Better than before, I guess. I don't want you to worry about me, okay? I'm still your tough ole dad. My head still feels pretty—*Jaicey?* Where are you going?" he called out after me, unable to move from his bed.

I was leaving the room. He of all people should know that I had to leave. *He'd done it.* After all this time, all the practice of *not* doing it, he'd done it anyway. Not on purpose, no, he probably hadn't even realized he'd done it, but he'd glanced at my neck, and that was enough. I was out of the hospital before I knew what was happening. I paced in the parking lot, my breathing labored. And then, there was Brayden. He stood in the parking lot, drinking Starbucks and staring into space with that goofy grin on his face.

"Hey!" He waved to me when he finally saw me, raising his cup in the air.

I stopped, out of breath. "What are you doing here?"

He handed me an extra cup that I hadn't noticed at first. "I came to see you. I heard about your dad. I thought you could probably use a friend."

I was going to remind him that he wasn't my friend, but I decided against it. That didn't really matter at the moment. "You mean to tell me you've been waiting out here all night? Why didn't you just come up?"

He smiled. "Well, it occurred to me, after I got here I might add, that I don't know your parents' names to ask for the room number. In fact, I don't even know your last name." He took a sip of his coffee, and I felt obligated to take a drink of mine as well.

I wanted to tell him that I didn't drink coffee; that it tasted disgusting to me and that it stunted your growth, but instead, I smiled and took a sip, feeling the warmth fill my empty stomach.

"Well, you shouldn't have waited. That's just insane."

He raised a brow. "Okay. That's sort of like a 'thank you' but different."

"Oh, uh, thanks. I do mean thanks. I just hate that you had to wait." I took another sip of my coffee, filling the silence.

He grabbed my hand and squeezed it gently. I flinched, without warning and without control. He didn't seem to notice. "You're welcome, Jaicey. I'm glad I waited."

He took another drink. "So, what happened? To your dad, I mean. Is everything okay? How is he?"

"He's—" I felt my voice catch before I could say more and chose to take a drink to mask it. I couldn't look at him, feeling sadness fill me up. It was too late. I felt the tears well up in my eyes.

Seeing me begin to cry, his happy expression faded. "Whoa, Jaicey, what is it? Is it bad?"

I opened my mouth to speak, but no sound came out. I shook my head, closing my mouth. He lifted his hand, ready to place it on my cheek, but I ducked out of his way, putting my hands up defensively.

"Look, I'm not even hurting you," he said softly. "I won't hurt you. I don't know what happened to you, what made you so scared…but not everyone's going to hurt you. I want to be able to touch you and not feel guilty for it."

I blinked; he was the first person who had ever stood up to me like that. "I'm sorry. It's just… I'm sorry." I shook his hand off.

He let go of my hand and took a drink of his coffee, unaffected. "Okay, let's go."

"Go? Go where? I can't *go*."

31

"Take a drive with me." He nodded his head toward the car, jingling his keys.

I shook my head. "I can't. I should really go back up to see my dad. I mean, thanks for the coffee and for coming, for staying. It's just that, he needs me right now. I shouldn't have even come down here."

"Take a drive with me." He looked at me seriously. "I didn't just propose marriage. It's just a drive in a car with a friend. Just come with me." I thought for a moment, chewing on my bottom lip. "Besides," he threw in, "that wasn't actually a question. You don't really have a choice."

He grabbed my arm, ignoring my cringe, and pulled me toward his car. It was parked pretty close to the building, so we didn't have to walk far. I knew better than to think Mom would be mad about me leaving with him—*if she even noticed*. She had her *Wife of the Year* award to earn. Her focus would solely be on Dad. Still, something bothered me.

"Wait a second, how did you say you heard about my dad again?" I asked as I climbed into his car, realizing there was no one else who knew.

"I didn't." He looked at me slyly. "I didn't say, I mean. I was out driving around, and some idiot pulled out of their driveway in front of me going really fast. We almost smashed right into each other. So, I followed them. I was going to give them a piece of my mind, you know, but they pulled into the hospital. The idiot was your mom. Then I saw a stretcher come out and get your dad. You looked so upset, all of you. I knew it had to be something bad. I figured you'd need someone to talk to."

"*And you've been here ever since?* Brayden, that was nearly twelve hours ago!"

He let out a small laugh. "No, no. Of course not. I went home last night. And then I went by your house this morning, and when I realized you weren't there, I came straight to the hospital. Your van was still there. I would've left eventually, I guess. But I knew you had to come out at some point. As it turns out, I was right."

"Why would you do that? Why would you wait all that time?"

"You know why, Jaicey. Because that's what friends do. I figured you needed a friend."

"We're not—"

"We *are* friends. Or at least, I'm your friend. No matter what you do or say, that's not changing. You can push me away as much as you think you want, but I'm not budging, okay?"

"But why?" I asked stubbornly.

"Because I said so." He sighed. "Because everyone needs a friend, and because one day you'll break and let me in, and on that day, I'm going to be standing right here. Still waiting. Probably old and decrepit by then, but still here." He smirked.

I didn't know what to say, and this time, when he grabbed my hand and squeezed it, I resisted pulling away. He held my hand as we drove for what seemed like an eternity. I was incredibly aware of the beads of sweat running between our palms, and I wanted nothing more than to let go, but I held on for his sake. He had been a good friend to me, after all. When he finally let go, he pulled the car over onto the shoulder and stopped.

"Uh, what are you doing?" I looked around, trying to figure out what he had planned. We were in the middle of nowhere, the highway stretching out for miles in front of us.

"I'm stopping," he said simply.

"Well, yeah, I can see that. Can I ask *why* you are stopping?"

"Because," he said with a wink, unbuckling his seat belt, "you are going to drive us home."

"What? What are you talking about? *No!* I can't. Let's just go home. I really don't want to," I told him, but he was already out of the car and making his way to my door. I spun around and pressed the lock down as fast as I could. He pounded on the window.

"C'mon. Open up, Jaicey," he said.

I shook my head insistently, but he continued to knock on the window patiently. "Open up, Jaicey. Open the door." He spoke slowly, like we had all the time in the world.

"Brayden, come on. Please don't do this," I begged him, panic setting in. "We are in the middle of the road."

"We're hardly in the middle of the road. I pulled over." He smiled, though we were clearly still partially in the lane.

"Seriously." I finally opened my door, frowning at him. "I don't want to drive. Come on, let's just go. Please." My heart pounded in my chest. I was amazed he couldn't hear it from where he stood.

He motioned toward the other side of the car. "Okay, let's go. You first."

"No! I mean it. I told you I don't drive. And I've never

driven this car before. I don't want to drive. Please, can we just go? I *can* drive. I just don't want to, honest. Ple—"

I stopped suddenly when I heard it, the roar of an engine behind us. I looked up and saw a green semi-truck headed right toward us. I swallowed and looked at him. He stood unwavering as the truck grew closer. My throat was closing up, and I feared I couldn't act fast enough to do anything. I was going to end up on one of those crime shows my grandpa always watched.

The driver was honking at us, the sounds growing closer and closer, but there was nothing I could do. It was seconds away, and we were clearly in the way. *"Brayden! Please! Please!"* I had no idea my heart could beat so fast. I thought quickly, leapt from the car, and landed on top of him just in time to see the truck whiz past us, honking, the driver cursing loudly out his window.

I kept my face buried in his shirt until I felt him shaking. I looked up and saw that he was laughing hysterically. I didn't know I was crying until saw the dark stains on his shirt. "You've got to be kidding me. What is wrong with you? Are you seriously *laughing?* Do you think this is funny?"

"No," he said through his laughter. "I, I mean, yeah. It *is* kind of funny. You should have seen your face."

I punched his stomach, making him double over. "It's not funny! We could have died."

"That's why it was funny. And we didn't die, now did we? Learn to live a little, Jaicey, gosh. What in the world do you have to be so afraid of?"

"I'm not afraid. I'm cautious. God, I just don't want to

die," I said forcefully, looking away from him as he continued to laugh at me.

Without warning, he immediately pressed his hand into my stomach and began tickling me. At first I was stiff, trying to push him away, but eventually I gave into laughter until my stomach burned, and I screamed, resting my face in his neck. As painful as it was for me to admit, he smelled good. *Really good.* The peppery cologne no longer seemed to bother me. I held my breath, trying not to breathe in his scent. I didn't need a reason to like anything about him. Finally, I rolled over onto my back and looked up at the sky. We were both quiet for a while, just staring into space.

He rolled over and looked at me, not saying a word, a small smile still on his lips. He looked from my lips to my eyes, then leaned a few inches closer. His eyes were so calming; it was easy to forget about everything else while staring into them. He grew closer, and suddenly, I knew what was coming. I threw my hands up to stop him. "So, um, we should probably get going. My parents will be wondering where I am." I interrupted the almost-kiss, moving myself out from under him.

He stared at me for a moment before recuperating, not a shred of embarrassment on his face. I, on the other hand, had to be nearly the color of a tomato.

"Okay, fine. But come on, then. If we're leaving, you have to drive," he said and stood up without saying another word.

I tried to protest, but he tossed the keys at me and climbed into the passenger seat.

Begrudgingly, I walked over to the driver's side and

opened the door. He snickered playfully as I scooted his seat up closer to the wheel to accommodate my short legs. *Not my fault I'm not freaking giant.* Okay, exaggeration. Brayden was probably five-foot-eleven, but when you're five-foot-nothing, everyone's a giant. I slid the key into the ignition, remembering this feeling. I stepped on the brake and slid the gearshift into drive, feeling my heart flutter. I stepped on the gas pedal. The car lurched forward with a start. Brayden laughed, obviously enjoying himself way too much.

"Woohoo!" he cheered, throwing his arms into the air as if he were on a rollercoaster as we gained speed. "Look at you, driving like an old pro! I guess you weren't lying after all."

I turned on my blinker, checking the lane and entering the highway smoothly. I stuck out my tongue, feeling a sense of happiness for the first time in what seemed like years. "I told you!" I could feel the grin on my face growing contagiously. In that moment, I felt it. I was letting him in. I was beginning to trust him; he had broken down a wall, and for a split second, that felt good. He laid his hand down, open, an invitation. I took one hand off of the wheel, and placed it cautiously in his, my skin tingling. He picked it up and pressed it to his mouth with a light kiss. I was completely out of my comfort zone, but I refused to shy away.

Suddenly, I heard it: the quiet, painful cries of a young girl. I saw the speedometer hitting 70, but *it wasn't fast enough.* I couldn't go fast enough. I felt my foot push the pedal *harder, harder.* My vision grew blurry, and everything in me hurt. *I could smell the blood.* I saw the headlights in my eyes, heard the honking horn, felt my whole body tense up. I heard her screams again, mixing with my own, heard the sickening crunch of metal on metal. Then came the explosion and the fire. It was everywhere, consuming my whole body, burning my hair and flesh. I felt my blood pouring from my body, soaking through my clothes. It was all I could do to move. I was in so much pain. My screams didn't even sound human. *Screaming. Screaming.* Someone was screaming my name.

"Jaicey! Jaicey!"

I jerked my eyes open and slammed on the brakes. The tires squealed and I was brought back to reality. There was no fire, no flames. The only screaming was my own. I shook in fear, afraid of what had just happened. It was a dream so real and vivid I could still feel the heat of it on my skin.

"Stop! Calm down! Stop! Stop!" He had unbuckled his seat belt and was out of the car before it had even completely stopped, running to my side. He jerked open my door and I fell out into his arms and onto my knees. He grasped my shoulders, shaking me, rubbing my head. "Oh my god, what's wrong? Please stop. *Please.* You're scaring me. What happened? What was that? I'm so sorry. I never should've—I should've listened—I'm so sorry." The words tumbled out of his mouth, making no real sense to either of us.

I couldn't speak, the vision still messing with my head. I collapsed into his arms and shook in a cold sweat. My breath pounded out of me like I had just run a marathon. Adrenaline coursed through my veins. It had felt so real; all of it. Tears poured down my face, mixing with my sweat. I just knew I was going to die right then and there if my heart didn't stop pounding so quickly.

He patted my back, rocking me back and forth and pressing his lips to my forehead. "What is it?" he asked. I shook my head, still unable to speak. I never wanted to speak again. Never wanted to feel that way again. My throat felt raw, as if I'd swallowed shards of glass.

"Jaicey, please tell me what happened." His voice was shaking, his breath warm in my hair.

"I don't know. I really don't know." I shook my head, repeating the words over and over again through my tears. "Please just take me home," I forced myself to say finally, in the calmest voice I could muster.

He nodded, pressing our bodies together and allowing me to calm down. "Of course," he promised.

When I finally stopped shaking, he picked me up like a baby and carried me to the passenger's side. I stayed nuzzled up to him until I was safely tucked down in the seat. I had never noticed how strong he was until that moment. He bore my weight effortlessly. He buckled me in with care, kissing my forehead once more without a word to acknowledge my flinch.

Once he was back to his side and buckled in, he spoke to me softly. "Are you sure that you're okay? I really think I should take you back to the hospital. A doctor should see you."

"I'm fine, thank you. Just take me home. Please," I said, then pulled my knees to my chest and forced myself to think of nothing at all until I drifted off to sleep.

CHAPTER NINE

S ometimes, I couldn't sleep at all. Other times, sleep
consumed me and kept me for its own.

When I finally woke up, I felt as though I had slept for
days, years maybe. Of course, my clock shone brightly on
the nightstand, reminding me of my inability to sleep past
4:04. I was lying in my bed with the covers tangled all
around me, drenched in sweat, my hair sticking to me. I
sat up, feeling the weight of the morning in my head. In
my sleep-fogged state, the light from the streetlamp
outside was like looking directly into the sun. I dragged
my feet out from under the covers and slid out of bed.

I walked slowly into the kitchen to find Dad sitting at
the table, staring at his hands. He looked up anxiously as I
entered the room.

"Jaicey!" He stood up to meet me, shoving his chair
back. "Oh, Jaicey! Thank God. We were so worried about
you." He held out his arms to wrap me in a hug. I
approached him slowly, willing myself to remain calm.
How much did he know? I couldn't even remember

coming home. It was as if my brain had shut down entirely.

"I'm fine, Dad," I mumbled into his chest. "Where's Mom?"

"Oh, she hasn't gotten out of bed yet," he said. *Right.* I had to remind myself that normal people didn't wake up as early as I did.

"Why are you up, Dad? It's early." I pulled back from him, staring at his face. I wondered if he'd been sick again.

"I couldn't sleep. I've been waiting for you to wake up." He sat back down and patted the seat next to him. I sat stiffly. "So, what exactly happened yesterday with that boy? Your mother and I don't know him," he said, his eyebrows raised.

"I don't know, Dad. He was just giving me a ride home." I wasn't exactly sure what Brayden had told them. After all, I'd only known him for a few weeks, but I already knew him to be an unnecessarily open guy. I really hoped he hadn't told them I'd been driving. "It's no big deal, honestly. He's just a guy."

Dad threw his hands up, surrendering. "Whoa, slow down. You don't have to explain yourself to me. I think it's great that you're back to hanging out with friends again. I've just never seen you with him before."

"Oh. Oh, yeah. Well, he's new this year. We've kind of been hanging out at school I guess. We have a lot of the same classes. We aren't really friends, though. I don't even know him that well."

He smiled. "Well, he seems like a nice boy. He was so scared when he brought you home. You should've seen

41

him. He carried you in all by himself. He really seems to care about you, Jaice."

"Yeah, well, I mean, he doesn't know me all that well." I couldn't look at him anymore, the past day's events rolling over me. I'd made myself look so stupid. It was mortifying to imagine what he must think of me.

"Your mom really liked him," he said, nudging me playfully with his elbow. I nodded. "Just promise me you'll be careful, okay? And bring him around once in a while, if you're going to start dating."

"We *aren't* dating." I stared at him, horrified by the very idea.

He gave me a confused look. "Well, you may want to tell him that."

"We're not dating," I insisted.

"Okay, but it's fine if you are. If not, that's okay, too. Put your guard down, sweetheart. There's no need to get upset. We're happy for you. We want you to have friends and hang out. He seems like a good kid. It may be good for you to start dating again, whenever you feel like you're ready."

"We aren't dating," I said again.

Dad nodded slowly. "I see. Well, I hope you don't mind, but your mom invited him over just as soon as you woke up. Dating or not, he was kind enough to bring you home safely after you passed out. I'd think you'd want to at least say thank you. We didn't raise you not to have manners." He stood up and left the room before I could protest.

I didn't want to call Brayden. I didn't want him to meet my family or be inside my house. This place was my safe zone. He shouldn't be here. I didn't want anything to do with him. What business did he have telling my parents we were dating...or even implying it? *We weren't dating.*

I grabbed my phone, ready to give him a piece of my mind, and dialed. He picked up on the second ring.

"How are you?" he answered, not bothering with a greeting.

"Just who the hell do you think you are?"

"Excuse me?"

"What did you tell my parents? Why do they think that we're dating? Huh? *Are you insane?* We are not dating, Brayden. I don't even know if we're friends. What could you possibly have been thinking? You had no right! *No right!* I can't believe you would do something so stupid."

There was silence on the other end of the line, so I went on. "You know, I've tried to be nice to you because you're the new kid and I guess I feel sorry for you, but you're really making it hard for me. I told you I didn't want to drive. I told you I don't want to be your friend. You either don't listen or don't care, but I am done, okay? I'm done with this little game that you're playing. Stay away from me. Stay away from my family. Leave me alone." I hung up, my heart pounding. I stared at my phone for five minutes, waiting for him to call back, even hoping a bit that he would. He never did.

CHAPTER TEN

That evening at just past five, a knock sounded on my door. "Come in," I called from my bed. My door slipped open slowly, almost cautiously, and I saw my mom's head peek around the corner, a giant smile lighting up her face.

"Jaicey," she announced, "you have a visitor."

"I, what? Who?" I slammed my book shut and eyed the door suspiciously. She stepped back and allowed Brayden to walk in. *Was he serious?* What was with this kid?

She smiled at me. "Dinner will be ready soon, you two." She shut the door behind her as she left without a second glance. She'd never left me in my room with a boy before. I guess she knew there was no chance of me acting like a regular girl anymore.

I stayed frozen on my bed while he lingered by my door. "What the hell are you doing here?" I asked, sounding braver than I felt.

"I came to see you," he said simply, running his hands

along the top of my dresser as if he were doing a white glove test.

"Why? Why would you do that? Why would you come here? I told you to stay away from me, Brayden. You can't just come showing up at my house, with my parents."

"Why not?"

"Because I don't want you to!" I whispered heatedly.

"Yes. Yes, you do," he said, walking toward me.

"I don't. I promise you I don't. I want you to turn around and leave and leave me alone." I folded my arms across my chest.

"Not unless you tell me why."

"I don't have to tell you why. I don't have to tell you anything. I don't even know you. Just leave." I stood up.

He took another step toward me, coming dangerously close. "Why? Jaicey, just tell me why. Tell me why you hate me so much and I'll leave. Not until then."

"Hate you?" I stopped, tilting my head to the side. "I don't...hate you. You brought me home and I'm grateful for that, okay? I don't hate you."

"But you don't like me?" he asked.

"But I don't like you," I confirmed. "You had no right to make my parents think that we were dating. You had no right to force me to drive your car. You had no right to come here tonight. It's just all too much and I don't need it in my life right now."

He reached for my hand, stopping my flinch before it could happen. "I'm sorry, okay? I'm sorry I told them that we were dating. I had no idea it would upset you so much. I was bringing you home passed out and they'd never met me. I thought fast and talked quicker. Okay? You had a freaking breakdown right in front of me. Christ, Jaicey. I was so terrified, out of my mind. I'm sorry that I didn't say whatever you had planned for me to say. I was just trying to do the right thing. No matter how you feel about me, *I do like you.* Don't ask me why because I couldn't tell you. I couldn't give you a single reason, honestly. You're stubborn as hell and rude and cold, but I like you. Everything about you. And I'd like to date you. So, what I told your parents wasn't a total lie. I would love to be lucky enough to date you."

"I don't—" I started to say, but he cut me off.

"*I know.* You don't date. You don't go to prom. You don't have friends. You don't drive. You don't talk. You don't like school. You don't leave your house. You don't tell anyone anything about you. I get it!" He twisted his mouth in frustration. "I get it and I don't care. I like you and I think that you like me too. You're just scared to admit it. I don't know why and if you aren't ready to tell me why, I guess that's okay, but I like you. I like you, I like you, I like you." He inched his face closer to mine, his eyes locked firmly on my lips. I was speechless.

"Brayden, please..." I tried to pull away but couldn't. His hand still held mine firmly and my stomach danced with butterflies.

"If you can look me in the eyes and tell me that you truly don't like me, not even a little bit, then I'll leave. You won't hear from me anymore. I won't bother you. I'm not a stalker. I'm just a guy. I'm a guy who likes a girl who won't give me the time of day." He laughed softly. "I see the way you look at me though, Jaicey. You don't look at me like a girl who doesn't have feelings for me, so tell me.

Tell me you don't like me and I'll leave." I was silent, not taking my eyes off of his. "Or...I could stay." He was less than an inch from my face now, the scent of his cologne burning my nose again. For the first time, I noticed the stubble around his chin.

"I don't...Brayden, I don't like you." I coaxed the words off of my tongue in succession. "I don't like you," I whispered, blinking heavily.

"Yes. You do." He touched my chin, his lips parting. I couldn't move. I watched his mouth grow closer to mine. My eyes shut instinctively. His warm breath hit my lips, and then his lips were on mine and we were kissing. His lips fit mine in all the right places and his tongue entered my mouth with passion. I kissed him back, though my heart pounded in fear. His hand caressed my cheek and I prayed he wouldn't feel the stray tear that escaped. And then, as quickly as it had begun, it was over. Just like that. He pulled back, his lips flaming red.

We were both silent, staring at each other, his hands still cradling my face. Nothing in my life had ever felt more right. I leaned in again, yearning for his lips. He pulled back, not far, just a few inches. I could almost taste him. My eyes begged for him to come back.

"You *don't* like me?" he whispered, his breath quick.

I shook my head, grasping at his face and pulling him to me. His mouth was back on mine and we were running our fingers through each other's hair. His stubble burned my cheeks, but I couldn't seem to care. In that moment, everything felt better. Everything felt good.

He pulled back again, a smile spread wide across his face. "Something you'd like to say to me, Miss Thomas?" I shook my head, leaning in for his kiss again. "Ah, ah, ah. I made you a promise." He held his finger onto my lips. "I said that if you told me you didn't like me, I'd leave. I'm nothing if not a man of my word. You've given me my answer, twice now. So, I'll just be going." He stepped back, his eyes daring me to speak up.

I watched him walk toward my door, the words hanging in my throat. His hand grasped the door handle firmly. He glanced my way one more time.

"Okay," I admitted, squeezing my eyes shut.

"Okay?" He let go of the door handle.

"Okay. You're right."

"I'm right?" he asked. I nodded. "What am I right about? You'll have to be more specific. I'm not positive I know what you mean." He smiled, but he was turning back to me.

"Brayden…"

He shook his head. "No. You have to say it."

My lips still burned from his kiss. My head swam with emotions I wasn't supposed to feel anymore. "I do."

"You do *what*, Jaicey? Three little words."

"I…like…you." I strained to say the words I'd never said before. Words I shouldn't say.

He placed his hand on the door handle once more, smiling from ear to ear. "Good."

"Good? Where are you going?"

He pulled the door open firmly, smiling. He tilted his head toward the hallway. "To dinner. Come on."

CHAPTER ELEVEN

My parents adored Brayden. Even my mother laughed more than I'd seen her in the past year. Everything was almost perfect and I had to admit, it almost felt good. Brayden's charms, it turned out, worked not only on me, but on my parents as well. He knew all of the right things to do: compliment my mom, joke with my dad. I could see it in their eyes, how happy he was making them. I had to wonder if my eyes would someday look like that.

"So, Brayden, you haven't told us where you're from. Jaicey says you are new to school this year," my mom coaxed.

"Well, all over really. My dad moved my family around a lot when I was growing up. I was born in Indiana. I lived in Kansas and Michigan briefly, but I've spent most of my life here."

"Here?" I was confused.

"Well, yeah. I grew up here in Lambert. I've been enrolled in private school my whole life though, until this year. My dad *finally* agreed to let me start attending public school."

"Private school, hmm? You must be very smart." My mom smiled.

"Thank you. My dad sure thinks so. He thinks very highly of education. He was always worried I wouldn't get the best education unless I went to an elite school. Lambert High sure proves him wrong, though. Half of my classes here are tougher than they were at Beattyville."

"So, your family lives around here, then? We may know them; what are their names?"

He took another bite. "It's just me and my dad. You wouldn't know him. He works for the government, so he travels a lot. Hardly gets around this town. He only moved here because of my mom. She grew up in Lambert. When she died, he couldn't bring himself to move us away."

"I'm so sorry to hear about your loss."

"Thank you," Brayden said stiffly.

"So, are you guys going to be going to prom together?" she asked, changing the subject shamelessly.

"*Mom!*" I blurted out, slamming my fork into my plate as my face grew red.

"What?" she asked innocently. "I just wondered. Why, it's only weeks away and it's your last prom. Surely you'll both want to go to it, right?" I covered my face with my hands, shaking my head.

"Actually, I may be out of town that weekend. I'm trying really hard to work around it, but it may not be possible. Jaicey has been really understanding about it. I was so worried she'd be furious," I heard Brayden answer, much to my relief.

"Of course," my dad said, speaking up. "That's our Jaicey. Are you going to see family?"

"Yes, my grandmother. We don't get to see her too often with my dad's work the way it is, so it's hard to reschedule when we do get the chance."

I smiled at him enthusiastically, my heart slowing. *He'd known to save me.* Somehow, he'd just known. "I told you, of course, I understand. I wouldn't want you to miss seeing your family, Brayden. *It will be fine, Mom.*" I put emphasis on the last sentence.

She nodded sincerely. "You're right. Forgive me, Brayden, if that came out a little too pushy. It was just an honest question. I hope you'll enjoy seeing your family."

AFTER DINNER, I walked Brayden outside.

"It was nice to meet you, Brayden, officially, that is. Are you sure you won't stay and have some dessert?"

He shook his head. "It was great to meet you both, too, Mr. and Mrs. Thomas. I'm sorry, though, I can't stay. Dad wants me home. He doesn't like for me to stay out too late on a school night."

My parents beamed at him. He was saying all of the right things. "Well, don't be a stranger," my dad called.

"Yes, you feel free to stop by any time." My mom waved as we shut the door.

I sighed once they were out of earshot. "Sorry about them."

"Don't be." Brayden laughed. "They're really sweet."

"They're annoying." I rolled my eyes. "So annoying. All of the time."

"They love you."

I smiled. "Yeah, they do. Though, I think after tonight they may love you a little bit more than me."

He shook his head. "You really think that went well? You think they liked me?"

"Of course. They, like, *loved you*."

"I hope so. I've never been very good with parents." He ran his palm over his face, his nerves showing for the first time.

"Are you kidding me? You blew them away."

He smiled. "You blow me away."

"Brayden." I slapped his chest playfully.

"I'm serious." He held out his hand. I took it as he began walking toward his car. He stopped as we got near it and kissed my cheek. "So, does this mean we're *officially dating?*"

I paused. "I don't know."

"What?" He looked shocked.

"I don't really date. You know that."

"Until now." He kissed my cheek again.

"I've said that I like you. Can't you just let that be enough for now?"

He shook his head. "It'll never be enough. Having all of you forever would never be enough." I looked at him, my eyebrow cocked. He smiled, his cheeks turning pink. "Okay, maybe that was a little too cheesy?"

I let out a loud laugh. "Seriously though, Jaicey. I told you I'd wait and I meant it. Just...be kind, okay? Don't keep me waiting forever." With that, he wrapped his arms around my waist. He kissed my forehead, my nose, and finally, my mouth. He kissed me gently, making my world spin. His kiss was perfect—it fit me perfectly, making me feel safe. My insides warmed at his touch. We pulled away slowly. He brushed his thumb across my cheek.

When I opened my eyes he was staring at me, a strange look on his face. "What's wrong?" I asked.

He smiled. "You didn't flinch."

CHAPTER TWELVE

The next week at school, as I walked out of my last class and into the parking lot, I was instantly met by Derek and his group of friends.

"Hey, Derek, how are you?" I smiled, trying to brush past him casually.

He held his arms out to stop me, refusing to move. "So, rumor has it you're dating the new kid."

I thought for a moment, narrowing my gaze. "And if I am?"

Derek looked hurt. "What is that supposed to mean?"

"I guess I am. We haven't really said anything officially. And why do you care, anyway? I don't owe you any sort of explanation."

"Jaicey, how can you say that?" His expression went soft, as if he really did care. *But why would he?* He and the other popular kids had always teased me. What had changed?

"What do you want, Derek? I'm just trying to get home."

He turned around to face his friends. "I'll catch up with you guys later, okay?" They nodded, mumbling their goodbyes and walking away. Then he turned back to me. "Just tell me this…are you going to prom with him?"

"No. I don't think so. He has something going on that weekend." I shrugged.

He took a deep breath, looking away from me for a moment. When he looked back, his jaw was firm. "I thought you had plans. I thought *you* didn't want to go."

"What? I mean, I don't want to go. I do have plans. He does, too. We aren't going."

"But you'd go with him, wouldn't you? If he asked you?" he asked, his eyes full of hurt. *Probably nothing more than a bruised ego.*

"Derek, please don't do this. I'm not your charity case, okay? It was sweet of you to ask me, honestly, but there are tons of girls who'd love to go with you. I'm sure Mallory told you to ask me, but honestly, it's fine. It's totally fine."

Derek's jaw grew tight again. I could tell he was starting to get more angry than hurt. "Stop it! Okay? *Stop.* And don't even suggest that I'd go with anyone else. I don't want to go with anyone else. I want to go with you."

"Derek…" I said, unsure of what else could be done.

"I don't trust him, Jaicey. I don't like him. No one knows anything about him. He's just *weird.* You're not like him. You're one of us."

"No one knows anything about him because no one will give him a *chance,*" I said, slamming my arms down to my sides. "That's how this school is. You and all of your friends sit around making assumptions and judging

55

people who are the least bit different from you. Well, guess what, Derek? I'm not anything like you. I'm different than all of you and I'm okay with that. Brayden has *made me* okay with that. So, yes, if I go to prom, it'd be with him, not you. You, who has never made any effort to talk to me until this year. You, who has treated me like crap every day of my life just because I'm not popular and not pretty. You have no right to talk to me about my life. You know nothing about me." I spat my words at him like venom, years of hate foaming out of me.

He put his fingers to his temple. "Jaicey, what the hell are you talking about? I've never *once* been rude to you. I've never been mean to you. I've done everything I know to do to *help* you. They said you needed space, so that's what I gave you. If I'd known for a second that this would be the outcome, I would've been with you every day. *Every single day.* I would've never left you alone. I'll never forgive myself for what happened. I'll never forgive myself for not being there. Just please…don't shut me out. Don't do this to me. I love you, Jaicey. I love you and I miss you so much." Tears were filling his eyes.

I looked at him, fighting back the urge to laugh. *What kind of joke was this?* Was he going crazy? He reached for my hand and I cringed, jerking it away. He pulled his hand back, a look of shock on his face. "Look at what he did to you, my beautiful girl. I should've been there. I'd do anything to have been there for you. I'm so sorry, Jaice. I'll never ever forgive myself."

He was starting to scare me. I took a step back. "I have no idea what you're talking about."

"Jaicey, please," he cried, reaching for me again.

"I really have to go, Derek." I pushed away from him and quickly walked toward Brayden's car, scared to look back to see if Derek was still watching me. I'd never seen him so upset.

"What was that all about?" Brayden asked as soon as we left the parking lot, glancing over his shoulder to where Derek must've still been standing.

"I really don't know."

He reached over, squeezing my knee. "You okay?"

"I'm fine," I promised him, though I wasn't sure myself.

"So, where to now?" he asked.

"Home." I sighed, staring out the window, still shaken up. "I just really want to go home."

"Okay, that's fine, but we have to make a slight detour first." He grinned and let go of my knee.

I nodded. "That's fine. So, how was your day?"

"Mine was wonderful. How was yours, *babe*?" He drew the last word out to see my reaction.

I wagged my finger at him, a giant grin spreading on my face. "Oh, no. Nope, you aren't allowed terms of endearment just yet."

"And when will I be?"

I thought for a second. "I'll let you know, how's that?" I giggled.

He smirked, tapping his fingers on the steering wheel. "Well to that I say, I guess you won't be getting your surprise."

"Surprise?" I sat up in my seat.

"Yep."

"What surprise?"

"*I'll let you know,*" he teased.

I slapped his arm. "Oh, you're *so* funny. C'mon, tell me."

"All right, all right. I'll have to show you, though. It's more fun that way."

Giving no other hint, he veered around a sharp curve and turned up the radio as we headed for the other side of town.

CHAPTER THIRTEEN

W hen we finally arrived at my *alleged* surprise, he
stopped the car and climbed out, rushing to my
side. I opened my door and looked around, trying to
figure out where we were. I had never been to this side of
town before, as far as I knew. There were small, white
houses as far as the eye could see. Brayden came to my
door and held out his hand. I placed my hand in his,
looking around. I didn't recognize anything. It was as if I
were in a whole different state, country even. Everything
seemed so...dirty. Abandoned.

"Brayden, what is this place?"

"You'll see," he replied. "Come on. Just keep up.
Follow me."

"But where are we? I've never seen this side of town
before."

"No more questions. Just come on," he whispered,
though I was sure we were alone. I hadn't seen a single
person since we pulled in.

"Just so you know, I know Taekwondo," I teased, poking him in the stomach.

He laughed, pulling me to keep up with him. "I'll keep that in mind."

We stopped in front of an adobe-style house. Its shutters were a faded blue, and the paint was beginning to chip around the edges. It was obvious that no one had taken very good care of the place in years, but it had once been a decent home. He led me up the porch and then pushed open a side door without knocking. Dust flew into the air as we entered the old house.

I gasped, coughing and waving dust from my face. "Brayden, are we allowed to be here?"

"Don't worry. No one's here. We're fine."

Though my fears weren't calmed, I stayed in step with him. It immediately became apparent that he had been there before. He led me through room after dingy room, each filled with its share of ratty toys and broken furniture. Finally, he led me down a dark hallway and into a small bedroom with a ladder square in the middle of the room.

I eyed the ladder suspiciously, noticing that it led up to a door in the ceiling. I wondered if it might lead to an attic. "What is this?"

"*This?* This is a ladder." He smirked, patting the wooden step.

I rolled my eyes playfully. "Gee, thanks. I got that much. I meant where does it go? What's it for?"

He shrugged. "Well, I don't know. I guess we'll have to go find out, won't we?"

I took a deep breath, placing my foot on the ladder

gently testing it to make sure it would hold me. The wood looked questionable at best. Before Brayden, there was no way I would've gone up that ladder. Before Brayden, there was no way I have even been in this situation. He had changed me. I was different, and I could feel it. I had known it deep down, but it became very obvious the moment I climbed up onto the first step. I felt his hands on my waist as I climbed, making it hard to focus on the actual climbing itself. As we arrived at the top of the ladder, I pressed my hand to the wooden door and shoved with all my strength. It was even heavier than I expected. I grunted, shoving it again. The door flew open with a loud bang, and I was surprised to see the sky.

The ladder had led us to the top of the house, which was flat and concrete. In the distance, I could see a hint of the lake, the sun setting behind it. I turned around to see him climbing up behind me. "Oh, Brayden. This is beautiful. How in the world did you ever find this place?"

He smiled out at the lake in the distance. "I didn't find it. This is my home."

I stopped, giving him a confused look. There was no way anyone could live in a place like this. Not now, anyway. The place seemed deserted. "You *live* here?"

"Lived here. This is where I grew up. That," he pointed down the ladder, "was my bedroom. This was my secret place. I'd come up here to work on my homework or to play. I'd just sit up here for hours. Sometimes when it was really nice I'd come up here and stay overnight, sleeping under the stars."

I didn't know what to say. This neighborhood was so different than the one I'd grown up in. All around me were dozens of rickety, abandoned houses. What could have once been a beautiful community was now an abandoned blemish in our city. It made me sad to picture him playing here all alone in this dusty place.

He smirked, reading my expression. "It's okay. You don't have to say anything. I know this isn't what you're used to and I get that. I just wanted you to see what I'm from."

"What happened here?" I asked quietly. "Why don't you live here anymore? Why doesn't anyone live here?"

"This place started falling apart: drugs, fights, gangs. It wasn't safe. My mom hated it so much. She didn't want me raised around all of it. My dad disagreed—said it would make me tough. He said it would make me brave. Eventually, my mom left. She just…left. We were all alone. I was seven. After a while, I think my dad realized that she was right and he moved us into town. We never heard from her again."

"Oh, Brayden…" I stared at him, pain emanating from his eyes.

He wouldn't let me comfort him. "No. It's all right. I didn't tell you this so that you would pity me. Me and my dad did fine for ourselves. He used to say, 'We're a team, you and I. You do what I say and it'll always just be you and me.' He was my best friend. We didn't always have a perfect life, but what we had was ours and I'm proud of it. I'm proud of him and of everything he did for me."

I bit my lip, unsure of what to say. "I'm sorry," I blurted out.

"You don't need to be sorry, Jaicey. I hardly remember my mom, and it was her loss, leaving us the way she did.

My dad took care of me. He did everything for me. I don't know where I'd be without him." He paused, staring into space. "I'm telling you this so that you can see who I am. I want you to know why I am the person that I am and why I do the things I do. We aren't going to be having dinner with my parents. We aren't going to all sit around the table and laugh and have fun. My parents aren't going to invite you over. That's not my life and that's not my family. I'm not anything like you."

My voice caught in my throat. He only knew the side of me he'd seen. He'd never know the true me. No one would. "I don't want you to think that my life is perfect, Brayden. It's so far from that. Things have happened to me. Horrible things. Things that have changed my family so much. My life isn't all that meets the eye, either. I don't expect you to be anyone but yourself. Nothing is perfect. I know that. You should know that I don't expect you to be anything you aren't."

He stared at me for a moment before holding out his arm and wrapping it around me. He rested his chin on my head. "Well, you're wrong about one thing. Some things are perfect. This right here, you and me, this is perfect." He stepped back, his hands on my arms. I looked down. He pulled my chin up, so I would look at him, and pressed his lips to mine. He kissed me the way I'd always wanted to be kissed. In that moment, I knew he was right. *This was perfect.* His lips covered mine, making my heart pound and my belly flutter. He wrapped his arms around me and held me until every wall in me crumbled. Just like that, I was his.

CHAPTER FOURTEEN

When I got home that evening, Mom and Dad were watching television in the living room. I shut the front door and they both looked up abruptly. Dad glanced at his watch and I saw him smirk.

"Hey, sweetheart," he called out.

I walked in and sat down between them. Dad threw his arm around me. *Flinch.*

"Where were you, Jaice? It's getting late," my mom said.

"I know. I'm sorry. I was out with Brayden. I didn't realize how late it had gotten."

"Wow, two nights in a row, right? Things must be going pretty well between you two then, huh?" my dad asked, a smile wide on his face.

"I guess so. We're just hanging out."

"So, is it official now? Is he your boyfriend?" he teased, poking his fingers into my side.

"No! God, Dad." I tensed up, pushing his hands away and fighting back laughter. "He's not my boyfriend."

"How is school going?" Mom asked.

"Fine."

"Anything new?"

"No, Mom. School is just school." I tried to hide the frustration in my voice.

"So, have you thought about going to the prom with Derek since Brayden can't go? I'm sure he wouldn't mind, and you know Derek would just be thrilled. I could talk to Rebecca about setting it all up."

I rolled my eyes. "No. I don't want to go. Even if Brayden could go, I don't think I would. What is your obsession with prom, anyway?"

My mom frowned. I'd obviously hurt her feelings. "Jaicey, why is it your instinct to hold everyone and everything at arm's length? I'm just trying to talk to you."

My dad spoke up, looking at my mom. "Jenny, let her be. She doesn't want to go. Let's just drop it."

Mom sighed loudly and took a sip of her coffee. Dad looked down at me and rubbed my nose. "We're proud of you, kiddo. We were always proud of you. We're just glad to see that you're starting to get back out there."

I looked down, laying my head on his chest, making sure not to let him see the small tear that ran down my cheek.

4:04, the same time every morning. My sleep always ended abruptly, as my breathing quickened and my heart pounded in my chest. I could never sleep past this time, no matter how exhausted I was. I rolled over in my bed and stared at the wall, begging my mind to allow me just a few more hours of sleep.

The house was silent, and in a strange way, I felt grateful for that. I hadn't realized how much I missed the afternoons where I'd come home from school and just sleep for hours on end, living in nothing but silence and solitude. Lately, everything seemed so loud. My mind was screaming at me for growing closer to Brayden, my parents were overjoyed that I was staying busy, and rumors, of course, were spreading like wildfire around the school about the two of us. It wasn't that I wasn't happy with him, of course I was, but everything was going so fast, and it had taken the quiet and darkness of my empty room for me to realize how much that scared me. The room's empty walls were beckoning to me, reminding me of the solace I used to find in them.

Finally, realizing I wasn't going to be falling back asleep, I gave up, rolling over and out of bed. I flipped on my lamp and was surprised to see a shadow lingering in my doorway. His eyes found me in the shadows. A scream escaped my throat and I instinctively pulled the covers up to protect myself. "What are you doing here?"

He held his hand up to quiet me. "*Shhh!* I wanted to see you. You don't think I notice that you always wake up at this time? I was out for a walk and I heard you crying."

"What are you talking about, *out for a walk?* It's four in the morning. And I'm not crying."

"It hurts me that you don't talk to me, Jaicey. You don't tell me anything. You aren't honest with me, always so quick to lie."

"Brayden, what are you talking about? I am honest with you."

"You never talk about that night," he said simply, his glare challenging me.

I gulped, the covers shaking in my hands. "What do you mean? What night?"

"You don't have to explain, Jaicey. I just wish you'd tell me the truth," Brayden said. "I'm here for you."

"What truth? What are you talking about?" I covered myself up to my chin as a cold chill ran down my spine.

"I know everything. I know what you won't tell me, what you won't tell anyone. Don't you see? I know what happened that night. I know your secret." His smile grew sinister as he stared at me.

I pulled the covers closer to my chest, my pulse quickening. "Brayden, you're scaring me. Please just go. We can talk about this later. My parents are right down the hall. You're going to wake them up."

"They won't wake up," he said simply.

"What do you mean? Of course they will. They're light sleepers," I said honestly.

Ignoring my statement, he went on. "Why don't you trust me? Why won't you just be honest with me about what happened? What's wrong with you?"

"I do. I do trust you, Brayden. I promise I do. It's just that it's really early and you're tired and I don't think you know what you're saying. You're confused. We can talk about this more tomorrow if you'll just leave."

"No. I'm not leaving. I'm not leaving until you tell me what happened. Tell me what you did, Jaicey. Tell me."

He started to approach me, his eyes cruel and menacing. I noticed the odd way he held one hand behind his back. It struck me then that he was hiding something.

"What do you have, Brayden? What is that?" I asked, trying to see what he was holding.

"I don't know what you mean." His voice was innocent enough, but it carried a strange quality I couldn't quite put my finger on.

"Behind your back. I can see that you have something. What are you hiding?" I squeezed the blanket until my knuckles were pure white, my whole body shaking furiously.

"Oh, you mean...*this?*" He pulled his hand slowly from behind his back to reveal a knife; a big kitchen knife like you'd use to cut up vegetables. It was covered in dark, sticky blood, dripping onto my tan carpet. A scream tore from my chest as I scooted back onto my bed, pressing my back into the wall. I covered my head with my blanket, waiting for death. No one would save me. I was alone. *He was coming.*

I shot up from sleep, beads of sweat covering my forehead. *It was a dream.* Brayden was nowhere to be seen. My alarm clock read 4:04. Same time every morning. I laid back down, trying to convince myself that it had all been a nightmare and that everything was okay. Shadows danced on my wall, tormenting my pounding heart. It all seemed so real. For a long time, I didn't move, afraid to glance at my doorway, afraid to turn on the light. Finally, when I had no other choice, I forced myself to sit up in bed and flip on the light, revealing an empty doorway. Just another day, I reminded myself. No one was coming for me. I was safe.

I hopped out of bed, still half asleep, and rushed for the shower, ignoring the hair that was still standing up on the back of my neck.

CHAPTER FIFTEEN

I was finally ready and about to walk downstairs. My copper hair was pulled up into a bun, I wore my favorite hoodie and jeans, and I'd even thrown a bit of mascara on for good measure. I had to guess I looked pretty decent today. Of course, there was no way I could ever truly know. We didn't have mirrors in our house. We hadn't for years. Everything we did was based on guesswork, and apparently, no one minded. Several times though, I caught my mom using spoons or the toaster to inspect her hair or makeup. I never used either. I never wanted to see what I looked like.

I was ready to leave when a loud sound rang out from the kitchen. I turned around to run back, startled by the commotion. "Dad?"

My mother was not far behind. "Chuck?" she cried as she ran into the room.

He was struggling to keep himself up off the floor, holding on to the counter with all of his strength, his face wrinkled in distress. I reached for his hands, but he waved me away forcibly, letting go of the counter and slamming onto the ground. A painful cry erupted from his throat. His face grew bright red as he began to cough loudly.

"Dad, here. Let me help you." I held my hands out, grasping just under his arms and attempting to help him stand. My mom followed suit.

"No," he shouted, pushing me away from him. "Just leave me alone!"

"I'm trying to help you," I said, straining against his weight.

He swung his arms out of my grasp. "No! One day, I won't be able to do anything for myself. Until that day comes, I want to do everything myself. Just go, Jaicey. You can't help me. Just go away."

I backed up, feeling like I'd been slapped. Mom took a step back, turning to look at me with a solemn face. "The doctor said there would be mood swings. You just have to understand that he's not himself right now, okay? He doesn't mean it," she said simply.

I could tell by her voice there would be no arguing. I nodded, walking hurriedly out of the room. I cast one last look back at my dad's angry face. As I walked out of the door, I heard my mom whispering to him. "Chuck, look at you." I heard her strain and knew she had helped him up. "We've already lost our daughter once. Don't you go and push her away any more than she's already pushed herself."

I shut the door hastily and felt tears collect in my eyes. I hurriedly brushed them away and sniffed. Then, I ran as fast as my legs would carry me, until my lungs burned. For the first time in a long time, I wanted nothing more than to be far away from the place I called home.

CHAPTER SIXTEEN

I could hardly focus on anything at school that day. My mind kept going back to what had happened with my dad. The episode this morning had made his tumor all the more real to me. His anger toward me, though I knew deep down that my mom was right, had broken my heart in a way it never had been broken before. My mind also kept drifting back to the nightmare I'd had. I knew that I had been stressed out over all the time I'd been spending with Brayden, but the nightmare had really bothered me, and I couldn't quite put my finger on why.

In third hour, I realized Brayden wasn't at school. He had seemed fine the night before, but he wasn't answering any of my text messages. I was worried about him as much as myself. It seemed as though everything that could go wrong, had.

When I got home that day, the house was empty. "Mom? Dad?" I called into the silence. There was no answer. It was eerie seeing my house so still. My parents so rarely left me at home alone anymore, I wasn't sure what to do with the quiet. I walked to my room and threw down my bag, then went to the kitchen and grabbed a bottle of water. Hearing my footsteps echo on the hardwood floor made me feel even more alone. I couldn't remember the last time I'd truly been allowed to be by myself.

I grabbed my phone and dialed Mom's number, but there was no answer. I walked back toward my bedroom, about to walk past their door when a noise stopped me. I pressed my ear up against the aging yellow door and waited. There it was again. Breathing, maybe? I couldn't be sure. I pushed the door open quietly and peeked in. He was lying on their bed crumpled into a ball, like I so often did when I was upset. He was turned away from me, toward the wall, but I could see his body shaking. At first I thought he may have been having another seizure, but I knew quickly that wasn't it. He was crying.

"Dad?" I asked, my voice so quiet I wasn't sure if he'd even hear it. He rolled over to face me, wiping his eyes quickly.

"Jaice? Sweetie, what are you doing here? I thought you'd be out with Brayden."

I walked over and sat down next to him on the bed, staring at him curiously. "No. He wasn't at school today. Dad, what's going on? Are you okay?"

He wiped his face again. "I'm fine, sweetheart. Listen, I'm so sorry about the way I acted this morning. I don't know what came over me. I can't believe how I talked to you. I never meant to upset you."

"Is that what this is about? Dad, no. Please don't even worry about that. I know you couldn't help it. Don't be upset over that. It's done now. I'm not mad at you. I'm just glad that you're okay now, that you're better. Please don't be sad."

"It's not just that. Jaice, listen, we went to see my doctor this morning. The tumor is progressing a lot quicker than they expected. He told me I can't work anymore. Apparently, it's too much of a liability to work with machines. The tumor…it's…it's already starting to win."

I felt a lump rise in my throat. I was unable to say anything. I had never seen my dad this way. Even sick, he'd always seemed so strong. Seeing him breaking down in front of me was devastating. "I just don't like not being able to support you and your mom. It's not who I am. You know that. None of this sits right with me, having to be taken care of," he said.

I rubbed his thinning hair gently. "It is okay, Dad. Mom makes plenty of money to support us. We'll be just fine. We just want you to focus on getting better."

He sighed, looking away from me. "Honey, I'm not getting better."

"What?" I asked, my voice shaking as I saw the gravity of what he was saying in his eyes.

"Your mother and I didn't want to tell you just yet, Jaicey, but I think it's best that you know. Even with chemo, the doctors just aren't very optimistic about how long I have. My tumor is inoperable. It's only a matter of time before…" He stopped, tears swimming in his eyes once more.

I choked back tears, my chin quivering. "That's impossible, no. No, Dad. You have to get better, you have to. I can't lose you."

He was crying again, rubbing my hand. "I might miss your wedding day. I might never meet my grandchildren. I might miss everything. That's my worst fear at this point, not getting to watch you grow up, not getting to see the woman you become. You're going to be a great woman, Jaicey. I have no doubt about it, but I'm your daddy. I'm supposed to be here to watch you. I'm supposed to help you; it's not supposed to be this way."

"It's *not going to be this way,* you hear me? You're going to be fine. You have to be fine."

He shook his head. "I need you to be strong for me, okay? And for your mom. She's going to need you to be strong. Don't be so hard on her. The next few years are going to be hard on us all, and I know she expresses her grief differently than you'd like, but she loves you. Jaicey, she loves you very much. We both love you more than you could possibly understand, sweetheart. You know that, right? You know that we love you?"

"I know. I know you do. I love you, too."

He placed his hand on my cheek and I tried to ignore his tremble as he ignored my flinch. "Ever since the accident, we've all been a little off, but this tumor has made me realize how messed up we are. It has made me realize that we can't stay this way. We have to get better. You have to start letting people in, honey, because if you don't, you'll stop being who you were raised to be. We raised you to love, and I know after everything that has happened it's hard for you, but you can't let him win. You have to be better. You have to promise me you'll get better. Your mom can't lose both of us. It'll kill her, Jaicey."

I looked at him, wiping a tear out of my eye. "Dad, listen to me. Stop this. You are going to be fine. We are going to be fine, do you hear me? This family will be fine." I kissed his nose.

"There's that brave girl I've missed." His chin quivered as I ran my hands through his salt-and-pepper hair.

"You've got your scared eyes on, Dad. Don't be scared, remember? I'm here. I'm here and nothing is going to hurt this family," I told him, tears now streaming down both of our cheeks.

"I love you, baby girl," he said with a chuckle, recognition in his eyes.

"I love you too, Daddy," I said, then leaned into his shoulder. I lay there until I heard his breathing slow and regulate. When he was fast asleep, I got up and went back to my room. My cell phone had three missed calls, all from Brayden. I called him back.

He answered on the fifth ring. "Hey, Jaicey."

"Brayden! Thank God, where were you today? I've been going crazy not hearing from you. Is everything okay?"

"Everything is fine. I've just been really busy."

"With what? What does that mean?"

"I can't say just yet, but if you want to know, you can come see for yourself."

"When? Now?"

"Well, yeah. Don't you want to see me?"

"Of course, I do. I'll come. Where are you?"

"The house I grew up in. The one that I took you to the other day. Do you remember?"

"Yes, I think so. What are you doing there?"

"It's a long story. How fast do you think you can make it here?"

"Just give me a little while. If I can try to catch the next bus I should be there in about twenty minutes, depending on traffic."

"Okay, hurry. I'll be waiting." I hung up the phone and grabbed my coat, leaving a note for Dad and heading out the door.

CHAPTER SEVENTEEN

I t seemed like the longest wait of my life. When the bus finally came, I jumped on anxiously and hurried to the closest seat I could find to the back. Once I got settled into my seat, I laid my head down on the cool metal of the window and wondered what Brayden could have in store for me. I desperately wanted to know. I was no good with surprises. That was something I thought he knew by now. As I sat there, waiting for my stop, I noticed an older man sitting across from me, staring in my direction curiously. He had to be in his late fifties with a plump belly, a graying head, and a kind smile. He glanced down at his phone screen and then back up at me. I smiled back at him softly, unsure of what to think.

"Excuse me, Miss," he said finally. "Are you J.C.?" he asked, putting unnecessary pauses in my name.

"Um, I'm Jaicey, yeah. I'm sorry. I don't believe I know you…" I offered him a small smile but immediately became nervous. My parents didn't like me riding the bus in the first place, and this guy was seriously creepy. What had I gone and gotten myself into?

"Oh." He laughed lightheartedly, waving his hand casually. "No, you don't know me. I have something for you. I knew it was you. He said you'd be pretty." He reached into his pocket and pulled out a folded up white slip of paper.

I took it from him, unfolding it lightly. Handwriting was scrawled across it in black ink.

When you arrive to the house, go all the way to the back, the last bedroom. You will see a hall to your right. Your next clue is waiting.

I looked up at the man, a quizzical look on my face. "I hope you don't mind," he said nervously, "but I read it. He never said I couldn't. I just wanted to be sure of what I was giving you." He sighed. "Young love, there's not a thing like it. Good luck, honey."

I smiled, not really sure what to say. Going to the house with Brayden was one thing, but going there alone to look for 'clues' was a completely different story. I waited patiently for my stop, my heart pounding as we grew closer. I watched the sun begin to set, trying to remember the night we shared on the rooftop. I wanted to make sure that I entered the right house.

I found myself staring at the map on the back of the seat in front of me and gasping. There was no bus stop in that area. I would have to get off at the next one. I picked up my phone, dialing his number hastily. It rang four times before going to his voicemail.

I slammed my phone down, frustrated and scared as the bus came to a halt. We were nearly two miles from my destination, but this was as far as I could ride. I stood up, trudging my way to the front, hand on my phone. *Please call back. Please call back,* I willed him silently.

I climbed down the bus stairs looking at the abandoned street. It was nearly dark, the streetlights would be on soon. I hadn't thought to bring a flashlight. Picking up my pace, I headed for the community where Brayden had lived, watching over my shoulder like a hawk. A man sat on a street corner with a suitcase and a cigarette.

I kept my eyes down, praying he wouldn't speak to me. He didn't, but that didn't make me feel the least bit better. A woman stood on a doorstep, pounding on the wooden door and screaming at whoever was inside. This was too much. I turned, racing back to the bus stop. He would just have to understand. I wasn't this girl. I wasn't brave. I couldn't do this.

As I arrived back at the bus stop, I checked the schedule. The next bus wasn't due to arrive here for another hour. I was stuck and stranded. I thought about calling my mom, but I knew she would be furious that I had gotten myself into this mess. Reluctantly, I realized my only choice was to find Brayden. To find him, I had to find that house. I sighed, accepting my fate and walking toward the sunset and ultimately, my fate.

WHEN I ARRIVED at the house I was pretty sure was Brayden's, I did as I was told. I entered, after knocking, through the side door. The sun had all but set, and the house was pitch black. I reached for a light switch, but as I had assumed, it didn't work. I failed to keep quiet, as I kept bumping into broken pieces of furniture. Finally, I pulled out my phone, using its screen for light. I walked down the first hallway into the last bedroom and turned to my right. Something moved in the corner of the room. I jumped, letting out a scream. It was a mouse, scurrying across the floor. This was all just too scary for me. How dare he do this? I looked around the second bedroom and hallway to no avail. The rooms were empty. I started to rush out when something caught my eye. I walked to the corner of the hall and bent down. It was a dust-covered teddy bear. It was so small I'd barely seen it. As I picked it up, I noticed the note pinned to its side. I pulled it off, dropping the bear.

Well done. I didn't know if you'd make it this far. Keep going, Jaice. I promise it'll be worth it. Your next clue: my secret place.

I pushed the note into my pocket and walked out of the hall, trying to remember what bedroom had been Brayden's. When I laid eyes on the old wooden ladder, I approached it and began to climb. I was seriously going to kill him for this. As I got to the top, I pressed the door open with a loud groan. It was even heavier than I remembered. I looked around, thankful to see the setting sun again. There was nothing to be seen. I glanced around the dusty roof, trying to see my next clue. Suddenly, I saw something move in the shadows below the house. I scrambled down onto my knees, trying not to be seen, listening. I tried to quiet my breathing, my heart pounding in my chest. Two cats began hissing down below, probably fighting for food.

Snap out of it, I told myself and pressed a button for

my cell phone to light up. I turned around, looking all over the roof for my next clue, and then I saw it. A plastic bike horn lay in a corner, a piece of paper attached to it. I ran over to it and picked it up, unfolding the clue. **Honk this**, it read, and then on the back, **Just do it**.

It was crazy how well he seemed to know me, to know my every thought. I did as I was told, honking the horn loudly. It echoed through the quiet neighborhood. I spun around quickly, expecting someone to be lurking in the shadows. Thankfully, no one was there. I was alone, though that brought me little comfort. In the distance, a dog began barking. I waited for something else to happen, anything else. That was all the paper said. I needed to get out of this house. I was done playing his game. I was tired and scared. The sun was completely gone, and every house in this community was empty. I ran down the ladder, heart pounding, and out the door as fast as my legs would carry me.

I had never claimed to be brave. He was asking too much of me. I ran until my legs felt like they were going to give out at any second. Somewhere in the distance, the dog was still barking and I knew I needed to find out where it was. There was no reason for a dog to be in this abandoned part of town, and once my head cleared, I wondered if this had been a part of his plan. I followed the barking past three more abandoned houses before my cell phone's glare finally made contact with the dog's glowing eyes. I jumped, letting out a scream. I slapped a hand to my mouth, looking around behind me. Seeing no sign of life, I walked up to the dog, a small terrier of some sort. It rolled over, displaying its belly proudly for a rub. I obliged.

"Who tied you up, boy?" I asked, the sound of my own voice sounding awkward in the night. I stayed crouched down, following the rope he was tied with to find it was attached to a wheel. I held my cell phone above it and realized that it was a bike. On the bike, was a note.

This was supposed to be a car, but I didn't want to press my luck. Find the light. Follow the light. I'll be waiting.

Was this a joke? He had to be kidding. I untied the dog and allowed it to run off into the woods, barking happily, and leaving me all alone in the dark once more. What was this light? I pulled the bike off of its tether and began to walk with it. I passed a few more houses on my way out of the community. There was no way I would go back. As I exited the subdivision and ended up on the sidewalk, I finally saw it. In the sky, way off in the distance, there was a beam of light, like the ones you'd see coming off of churches.

I sighed, eyeing the bike. I hadn't ridden a bike since I was ten, and I was still a bit wobbly as I climbed on, but I wanted more than anything to get far away from this part of town and I knew the bike was my best bet. I followed the light down the road and through a few more communities. When I finally saw people, my heart rate slowed a bit. I pedaled faster, ignoring the questioning stares of faces under the street lights and promising myself that once I found Brayden, it would all be worth it. Of course, that was before I ended up at the entrance to a patch of woods. The light was just beyond the trees, but I knew if I went through them, I would lose it.

I sat still for a few minutes, just staring at the trees. I tried his cell again. No answer. At this point, I was furious. I put my cell phone back into my pocket and stared at the light. It was straight ahead and slightly to my left, but how deep into the woods? What if I passed it because I lost sight of it in the sky? What if it went off? Without options, I was forced to make my way toward it. I pressed my feet to the pedals, pedaling as fast as I could, veering around trees and bumping over rocks. Lucky for me, the patch of woods was misleading in its depth. I was out before I knew what hit me.

I stopped as my bike tires slid into sand and I could see the light source. I realized in awe that I was on the lakeshore, staring at a lighthouse. I thought I had been here before, but I couldn't be sure. I hopped off the bike and laid it down carefully on the sand, rushing toward the lighthouse. I pulled my cell phone out again and noticed it was beginning to die. I dialed his number, adrenaline coursing through my veins. If he didn't answer, I'd call my mom. I was going home. I wouldn't stay here one second longer.

The second it began to ring on my end, I heard his ringtone in the distance. "Brayden?" I called out, my voice unsteady. "Are you there?"

He didn't answer. I followed the sound of his ringtone to a pile of large rocks. I saw his phone lying on one and picked it up. My face was on the screen as I hung up. I looked around the shore, really starting to worry about him. "This isn't funny!" I shouted.

Out of the corner of my eye, I saw a flicker of light. I walked closer to it and saw three small candles. Someone cleared their throat behind me. I spun around on my heels, ready to run, and there he was. He smiled his playful, carefree smile. "Well, it took you long enough!"

My anger was instantaneously forgotten and my fear washed away. I ran up to him, leaping into his arms. *"Are you crazy? Do you know how scared I've been? You can never ever ever do anything like this ever again!"* I kissed his lips fiercely.

"Awe, poor baby," he taunted, pulling away. "I didn't expect you to take so long, I didn't realize it would already be so dark." He kissed my cheek gently, squeezing me into a hug.

"Well, it was. It was dark and scary." I realized how childish I sounded but I didn't care.

"Well, I'm glad you came, you brave, brave girl." He patted my head, puckering his lips out. "And I'm glad you survived our *treacherous* town. Now, for your surprise."

"Surprise?" I asked.

He turned me around and leaned down to whisper in my ear. "Close your eyes, pretty girl."

I did as I was told. I heard him fumbling with something and then I felt warmth hit the front of my body.

"What are you doing?" I asked.

"Patience," he said calmly. "Okay, now you can open." He was standing far away from me now. When I opened my eyes, I gasped. Fire. Candles, actually. There was a large patch of candles sitting in the sand. He walked up to me and grabbed my hand, lifting me to stand on top of a large rock.

"What are you doing?" I asked, growing more confused.

"Look at it now." He pointed to the ground, I stared down. Looking at the candles from up above showed something I hadn't been expecting. I covered my mouth in shock. He'd used candles to spell out the word 'PROM?' in the sand. It was a question. My jaw dropped. I looked over at him as a goofy, hopeful grin spread to his face. Unsure of what to say, I jumped down and hugged him.

He spun around in circles, holding me close. "Ha, and I thought you weren't interested in prom."

I shook my head. "I never said that."

"Actually, you did," he assured me.

"I said I wasn't interested in going to prom with *Derek*. There's a difference in that and not wanting to go at all," I told him matter-of-factly, feeling practically giddy.

"So, is that a yes?" he asked, exasperated.

I looked into his dark eyes, watching the reflection of the flames dancing in them. "That's a yes."

He kissed me gently at first and then more fierce, scooping me up and carrying me to where a blanket had been laid on the sand. He sat beside me.

"So, whatever happened to visiting your grandma?"

He kissed my cheek. "We never visit my grandma."

"But you said—"

"Well, I couldn't very well give away my entire surprise, now could I? Besides, you wouldn't have said yes back then. I had to wait until I knew you'd say yes," he said slyly.

"So, you've had this planned all along? This whole time? Even that night? When we weren't even dating?"

He ran his hands through the sand, picking up a small

handful and tossing it in my lap. "I was dating you long before you realized it, Jaicey Thomas."

I kissed him then, rolling over to lay on top of him. "So, when did you plan it? How did you plan it?"

"A man never reveals his secrets," he told me, his lips brushing mine. "But I started planning as soon as you turned down Drake. I just had to figure you out first."

I smiled at him. "His name's Derek."

"Huh?"

"*Derek*, not Drake. His name is Derek, you dork."

"Oh, is that right?"

I laid my head on his chest, giggling. "Yes, that's right."

"That's it!" He stood up, bellowing playfully and throwing me over his shoulder, racing toward the dark water. I screamed, laughing as he bounced me across the shore. I braced myself for the shock of the cold water to hit me. When it did, I gasped only seconds before I was submerged, laughing even once I hit the water. I had never felt anything so cold, but it didn't matter. Nothing mattered. I pushed up out of the water and grabbed his shoulders, shoving him under the water, too. He came up, his shirt sticking to him, and splashed me. I splashed him back.

"Oh, now you're going to get it," he warned, picking me up and holding me above the water.

I shrieked, grasping for the water. "No! No! I give up! You win! I give up!"

He brought me back down, our bodies sliding together, and I threw my arms around his neck, pulling him into a kiss. His kiss warmed me despite the icy spring water.

He pulled away, looking at me. "My God, I love you."

I stopped laughing and swallowed hard. Water dripped into my eyes, but I couldn't move. "What?"

He wiped water from his face, shock filling his expression. "S-s-sorry. I mean, I meant that to be so much more romantic, but it just slipped out. I love you, Jaicey. I'm so completely in love with you."

"I, um, wow." I didn't know what to say so I chose silence. The cold of the water was starting to hit me and I began to shiver.

He put his fingers over my lips, leaning down until he was only inches from my face. "Don't say anything. Not now. Don't feel pressured. I waited for you to let me in, and you did. I waited for you to admit your feelings, and you did. I waited for you tonight, and here you are. So, I'll wait. I'll wait for you to love me...because you will. And you are so *completely*...worth the wait."

Before I could say anything, he kissed me gently and then dunked me under the water's surface.

CHAPTER EIGHTEEN

When I got home that night, mom was lying on the couch. She didn't look up as I walked into the room. I walked over and laid my head on her lap. She placed her hand onto my sopping head and then removed it, staring at her palm. "Jaice, why are you all wet?"

I yawned. "I was hanging out with Brayden. We went down to the lake."

"Jaicey, it's April. What on earth were you kids thinking? You can't go swimming this time of year. You'll make yourself sick."

I sat up and looked at her. "We dried off."

"Look at you. Your hair is a soaking wet mess, and your clothes…" She felt my face, her jaw dropping open. "You're practically an ice cube. Come with me."

I stood, following her into the bathroom where she grabbed a towel. "Take your clothes off and get dry. I'll be right back with something warm." She shut the door behind her.

I did as I was told, stripping each piece of freezing, wet

clothing off of me and rubbing my skin with the towel until I was completely dry. She opened the door back up and handed me a pile of clothes. "Put these on when you're done." She didn't look at me. I wasn't sure if it was out of respect for my privacy or annoyance.

When I was dry and dressed in fresh clothing, I opened the door. She was still standing there. "Hand me your clothes so I can throw them into the wash, and then we need to blow dry your hair."

I handed over the clothes and my towel and walked back into the bathroom. After a few minutes she was back, blow dryer in hand. She plugged it in and turned me around, pointing the dryer at the back of my head. The warmth felt amazing on my cold body. I shivered as she continued to dry me, finally realizing how cold I was. When she was done with the back, she turned me to face her, drying my hair carefully so as not to burn my skin. She ran her fingers through my hair, holding each piece carefully as if it were made of glass. She watched my face as she dried me, staring at me intently.

"Your lips are blue. You know, you should really be careful down there. The lake can get pretty dangerous at night."

"We were fine." I nodded. "I swear we were fine."

She laughed. "You know, your father and I used to go down there."

"You did?" I asked, so thrown off by this change in attitude.

"We sure did. We were your age once, too, you know. We used to love going down there. We even took you a few times when you were little. Do you remember?" I thought back. I really couldn't remember. "You were really young. I guess you probably wouldn't remember." She shook her head.

"Did you ever go by the old lighthouse?" I asked.

"Lighthouse?" She paused. "No, I don't remember any light house. We typically stayed to one particular place that we knew, but I've been up and down that shore. I never even seen a lighthouse."

I shivered. "That's where he took me."

"Well, it's been a while since I've been there. It may be privately owned, too, or I may have just missed it. Who knows? You guys just be careful, okay?"

I nodded, too tired to protest. She shut the dryer off, running her hands over my hair one last time. "Okay, you're all good."

I yawned, following her back into the living room and laying my head on her lap once she'd sat down. I just didn't want to go to bed yet. She didn't seem to mind, so I closed my eyes. When I was so close to sleep I could taste it, I felt her hand rubbing my hair as she had so often done when I was growing up. That was the last thing I thought of seconds before sleep found me.

4:04, the same time every morning. I shot up off the couch, panting. I looked around the room, unsure of where I was. Mom had stayed there with me all night. She was lying at one end of the couch and I was at the other. At some point during the night, she had laid a blanket down over both of us, our feet sticking out at both ends.

She stirred, still half asleep. "What is it, Jaicey? What's wrong?"

"Nothing, Momma," I assured her. "I'm fine. I'm going to go grab something to drink. Go back to sleep."

She laid her head down on command. I got up quietly, careful not to disturb her. I started walking toward my bedroom, but something made me stop in my parents' doorway. There lay my dad, his television still on, just like always. I remembered crawling into bed with him and my mom when I was little and I'd had a bad dream. Without thinking too much, I walked into the room quietly and lay down next to him, trying not to wake him. He slept soundly, and for the first time ever, I fell back asleep.

CHAPTER NINETEEN

When I awoke the next morning, I had two lumps on either side of me. I opened my eyes and saw my mom and dad both staring down at me, their faces far too close for comfort.

"Ahh! The creature lives," my dad teased. "You were snoring like a horse."

I laughed, rubbing sleep from my eyes. "A horse? Dad, horses do not snore."

"You were snoring like your dad," my mom added.

I snorted, to which my dad objected, "*Hey!*"

We laughed, loudly and together, for the first time in ages. I think each of us knew that something was different that day. Something felt like the old us.

"So, who wants IHOP?" Dad asked.

I thought for a minute, yawning. "I think I have a better idea."

"ALL RIGHT, one whooping heap of Chuck Thomas's world-famous pancakes coming right up," Dad said as he placed the plate loaded with pancakes on the table. I looked around at the huge amount of food we'd managed to whip up.

"Let's eat," Mom cheered happily and handed us each a plate.

We hungrily dug in, each loading up their plate with a mountain of food. "So, Jaicey, how was your night last night?" Dad asked, taking a bite of his eggs.

I swallowed my toast. "It was really, really great. Actually, it started out kind of terrifying. Brayden had me go on this scavenger hunt down by the lake."

"A scavenger hunt? You didn't tell me that! That sounds exciting," Mom said happily.

"It was exciting, but creepy. It ended up getting dark before I was finished so it was kind of scary, but it ended up being really sweet."

"So, what was the prize?" she asked, her face curious.

"Oh," I said. I had been waiting for the moment to tell her. "Well, actually, it ended at the lake. There was this old lighthouse, and he took me over by these rocks where he had a whole bunch of candles set up."

My dad grumbled in disapproval. "I don't like the sound of that, Jaicey. You shouldn't have been wandering around after dark alone. And the candles, that could've been really dangerous."

"We were really safe, Dad. I promise. Brayden was careful with the candles, and he didn't mean for me to be alone after dark. It was just a timing issue. Anyway, at first I thought it was just a bunch of candles and then from up

95

on top of the rocks I could see that he'd spelled out 'PROM?' in the sand!"

Mom nearly spit out her orange juice. Her eyes bulged. "*What?* He asked you to prom?"

I nodded. "Yeah. Apparently, he had this whole thing planned out the whole time. He just really wanted to surprise me."

"*Jaicey Paige!* I can't believe you waited this long to tell me. I wish you would've taken pictures. That sounds so sweet. Oh, but we have to get you a dress. We have so much to do. Prom is in, what, a week?"

"It's next Saturday, yeah. I hope we can still find a dress in time."

"The boy sure does know how to keep you waiting," Dad threw in, obviously unhappy about something.

"Chuck, it's fine. Why, we can go today if you'd like, Jaice. What does your day look like?"

"I'm free all day, but don't you have a closing today?"

She waved her hand casually. "Oh, Connie can take over. We've got a prom to get ready for! What do you say, Dad? Are you up for a day of shopping?" she asked him excitedly, her jaw hung open.

I looked at my dad, his mouth still full. He looked back and forth between us and then swallowed. "Oh, uh. Well, you know, shopping isn't really my thing. I'll probably just stay here and clean up breakfast. You girls go, though. You'll have a nice time."

I smiled. "And by clean up do you mean eat all of the leftovers in sight?"

"No." Mom laughed. "He means he doesn't want to carry our bags all day."

"Actually, you're both wrong." Dad looked at us seriously before cracking a smile. "I meant both."

We laughed. Mom smacked my leg playfully. "Well, come on, then. Hurry up and finish your breakfast and we'll head out. We have a full day ahead of us."

I took another bite of bacon, grinning from ear to ear. My mom was back.

CHAPTER TWENTY

M om and I shopped nearly all day, at every store in our town and three towns over. I knew I'd found the dress the second I laid eyes on it, but Mom insisted that I try it on.

"You'll want to make sure it fits you right, Jaicey."

I walked into the dressing room and stopped when I saw the mirror. I turned to leave, instinctively, but stopped myself when I saw my mom's face. I hadn't seen her this happy in a very long time. I closed my eyes, forcing myself back into the small room and facing a corner. We had made such progress lately. I wouldn't be the one to mess that up. I stood in the corner, as far from the mirror as possible, and slipped the dress over my head. I zipped it up on the side and stepped out of the room.

My mom gasped when she saw me. The red dress wrapped around my chest and stomach tightly, hugging my hips. As it neared my legs it flared out in ripples, stopping just short of my feet. She walked up to me, pulling my hair around to the front. "You look so pretty," she said simply, her hands clasped in front of her mouth.

"So, you like it?"

She nodded. "Jaice, it's perfect."

"Okay," I said. My mom had been waiting for this moment for so long, and it felt good to finally give it to her. "I'm going to go take it off, then."

She nodded, not saying anything else. I rushed back to the dressing room, pulling the dress off, careful not to glance toward the mirror. I hung it back up on the hanger and hurried out of the room.

When I walked out, Mom was holding a white sweater. "Do you want this too? To cover up?" She looked at me awkwardly. She didn't want to say what we were both thinking.

I took it without needing to tell her how much I needed it. "Thank you, Mom."

She smiled at me, placing the sweater in the cart. "So, this is the one? You're sure?"

I nodded. "I love it. This is the one."

"We can try on a few others if you'd like. I'm in no hurry."

"This is it," I swore to her as we made our way toward the checkout lane.

After we paid and were preparing to leave, I heard a voice cry out behind us. "Jenny Thomas! Is that you?"

We turned around to see Rebecca Anderson hurrying our way, and much to my dismay, Derek was following behind.

"Rebecca! How nice to see you!" My mother gathered her into a friendly hug.

"Well, it is good to see you, too. It has been too long."
She laid her eyes on me, joy radiating from her face. "Oh
my god, Jaicey!" She outstretched her arms and grabbed
me quickly. I flinched, then tried to hide it by patting her
back.

She let go of me, obviously embarrassed, her gaze
flicking toward Mom's for a second. "It is so good to see
you, sweetheart. Oh, we've missed having you around.
How are you?"

"I'm good, Mrs. Anderson, thank you. How are you?"
Smile.

She pursed her lips. "Oh, what's this *Mrs. Anderson*
nonsense? You can still call me Rebecca. I know you and
Derek aren't together anymore, sweetheart, but that
doesn't mean you're any less a part of the family than you
were before."

Derek looked at me warmly, a small, sad smile
crossing his face. "It's nice to see you, Jaicey. Jenny."

My mom wrapped her arms around Derek, hugging
him for a little too long. She whispered something in his
ear, though I couldn't be sure what it was.

"How's your father doing? I heard he was in the hospital," Mom addressed Mrs. Anders—I mean, Rebecca.

"Oh, he's all right, thanks for asking. Just a minor fall.
Ever since Mom passed last year, he's just not in too good
of health, bless his heart."

Mom nodded, clutching her chest. "I'm so sorry to
hear that. We've been thinking about him. I hope you'll
tell him I asked about him."

"Of course. He'll be happy to hear that. He always

loved you...*both of you.*" Rebecca smiled at me. "It was just so good to see you. I know Derek feels the same way."

I nodded, feeling increasingly uncomfortable. I watched Derek glance at my dress. "Is that for prom?" he asked cautiously.

Both mothers looked uncomfortable. I spoke up softly. "Yes, it is."

He looked down. "Mom, can we please go?"

"Of course, sweetheart," she said dotingly.

"Good to see you, Ms. Thomas. Jaicey." He ducked his head and walked away quickly before we could say anything else.

Rebecca looked at me sadly. "You'll have to excuse him. He's been having a really rough time with everything. I know he was glad to see you, honey. We're all just so glad that you're all right." She looked to my mom. "Call me sometime, Jen. We'll meet up for brunch and catch up."

Mom nodded. "Take care."

With that, she was off, chasing after Derek, who had already disappeared. Mom led me out of the store quickly. Once we were in the car and on our way home, I looked to her.

"Mom?"

"What, honey?"

"What did Mrs. Anderson mean when she said that Derek and I aren't together anymore?"

"What are you talking about?" she asked, turning down the radio.

"She told me to call her Rebecca. She said that just because we weren't together anymore, Derek and I, that I

101

should still call her that. What did she mean? Derek and I were never together."

My mom was quiet for a moment, pursing her lips. "I'm sure you just misunderstood her."

"No. I don't think so. That's not all. Derek has been acting really weird toward me lately."

"Sweetheart, I'm sure you just misunderstood. You know Rebecca and I went to school together. We were very close. You and Derek used to play together as children and have grown up together. I'm sure she just meant that you don't have to call her Mrs. Anderson like you're a stranger. That's all."

"So, you didn't hear her say that?" I asked. She was quiet, staring ahead. "Mom?"

She looked at me for just a second before turning the radio back up slightly. "No, Jaicey. I didn't hear her say that."

I sighed, staring out my window, not completely sure I could believe her.

CHAPTER TWENTY-ONE

When we got home that night, I called Brayden. "Hey, guess what I did today?"

"I don't know. What?" he asked, sounding distracted.

"I bought my dress for the prom," I told him, excitement filling me. "Oh, and it's beautiful. You're just going to love it."

"I'll love the girl wearing it," he cooed.

I laughed. "I'm serious. It's amazing. I can't wait for you to see it."

"I can't either. Saturday's the big day."

"You could come over before that, you know. Whenever you want. If you want to see it sooner, that is. I mean, I could ask about you coming tonight."

"Actually, I'm in the middle of something here. Maybe another day though."

"Oh, okay," I said quietly.

He cleared his throat. "I do want to see it though, Jaice. I wish I could be there right now."

I smiled. "Want to hear a secret?"

"Of course," he said.

"I'm actually kind of excited for prom. Really excited, honestly. I never thought I'd say that."

"Well, look at that. You are normal, after all. I'd been worried about you for a while," he joked.

"I'm serious." I laughed at him, my stomach dancing with every word he said.

He laughed back. His laugh made me smile brighter. "You'd better be. Believe it or not, I actually have quite a night planned for you."

———

4:04 AM. I shot up in bed, heart pounding. My throat was dry and itchy. I looked around the room, checking carefully for shadows. There was nothing. I pulled the covers back, shivering as the cool air hit my body. I stood up, tiptoeing toward the kitchen to get a drink. As I got closer to the end of the hall, I noticed my parents' bedroom light shone underneath their door. What on earth were they still doing up?

As I drew closer, I could hear their hushed tones.

"I don't know what you want me to say, Jenny. You know what the doctor said. We have to stick to the plan. This was our decision, not just mine. It's what is best for all of us, and more importantly, it's what's best for her. We don't have a choice in this now."

"It's just so hard, Chuck. It wasn't supposed to take this long; they never said it would be *years*. Days, weeks, even months, sure; but this? How am I supposed to keep it up?

And for how long? Forever? Do you really think we can do that?"

They were talking about my dad's tumor again, I was sure. I didn't want to eavesdrop but I just had to know what was going on. I knew there had to be things they weren't telling me, things they thought would be too hard for me to hear.

"We will keep it up for however long it takes, however long she needs us to. Doing anything different than what we've been doing could just set her back even further. We're doing the best we can for her."

"Chuck, you didn't see her today. You didn't see how confused she was. It was the hardest thing I've ever done —lying to her like that."

"I didn't see it today, no, but I've seen it before. I know how it is. Why is this any different than any other time?"

"Because it was Rebecca…and it was *Derek*. And how I am supposed to explain to them what's happening? They love her as much as we do. It's just not fair."

"I know you love the Andersons, Jen, but this is not about them. This is about our daughter. This is about what's best for Jaicey. They understand that."

"How can they possibly understand that? I don't even understand it. How can I be expected to lie to our daughter every single day of her life? Possibly for the rest of her life. How can any of this be the right thing?"

"You know what the doctor said. He said we have to let her work through it. We couldn't force her then and we can't force her now. It'll only be worse on her. Besides that, as far as I'm concerned, she's better off not knowing."

"You can't believe that." My mother's hushed tone sounded as if she were crying.

"You're damn right I can," my dad said.

"Chuck, she doesn't remember anything. It's not just what happened. She doesn't remember a thing about who she was."

"She's our daughter, Jenny. That's all she needs to know. We made this decision a long time ago. You can't just change your mind now. It's done."

I heard footsteps then and rushed from the door, careful not to make any noise. I huddled in the kitchen, trying to come up with an excuse as to why I was up. After a few moments, the kitchen light flicked on.

"Jaicey?" my mom asked.

Keep your voice calm. "Hey." I faked a yawn.

"What on earth are you doing in here?"

"I was thirsty. I came to get a drink."

"In the dark?" she asked, her eyebrows raised.

"I didn't want to wake you up."

She walked to the counter and grabbed a glass, flipping the faucet on.

"Sit down, Jaice," she told me.

I did, my heart hammering. She brought my glass over to me and set it down, scooting it toward me. "There you go." I took a sip, careful not to let her see my hands shaking. "Are you sure everything is all right?"

"Everything is fine. I just woke up thirsty." I smiled, taking another drink.

She watched me drink until the cup was empty, her face saying she didn't believe me. She took the glass back, refilling it and bringing it to me once again. "Feel better?"

I nodded. "Why don't you go on up to bed, then? Take the cup with you in case you get thirsty again," she said.

I nodded, grateful for the chance to leave. I picked up the glass, hurrying back to my room.

When I got to my room I shut my door, sliding down the wall. My whole body shook with fear. What on earth was going on? What were they talking about? Had I really forgotten who I was? How could I? *Who was I?*

Questions swam in my brain as I began to drift off to sleep again. When I woke up the next morning, the cup was gone from my nightstand and the prior night was a bit of a blur. Had it all been just a bad dream?

CHAPTER TWENTY-TWO

Tuesday at school, Mallory found me after third period. "Jaicey Thomas, *girl*, please tell me what I've been hearing is true."

I smiled, already knowing what she'd heard. My smile was enough confirmation. "You and the new kid, huh? So, that's why you said no to Derek, then? I always knew you knew how to keep a secret! I can't believe you didn't tell me." Her smile was playful as she waited for me to spill the latest gossip.

"No, it wasn't why I said no to Derek. I swear. Brayden and I are fairly new. It definitely hasn't been a secret."

"Budding romance? Oh, our Jaicey is back. This is so exciting. You have to tell me *everything*. Every detail. You know how I am." She held her hands out, wiggling her fingers as if pulling information from me.

"I will." I nodded.

"You have to. Today. After school, then?" she begged. "I'll just die if I don't know soon."

I started to make an excuse to say no, thinking quickly.

"Please don't say no. Please. Just one night, Jaice." She pushed out her bottom lip.

"Okay," I said, regretting it immediately.

She stifled a scream, hugging me tight and jumping up and down. "Yes! We can just ride home after school together. We'll take my car." She ignored my flinch, for which I was grateful.

"Oh," I said. "Actually, Brayden usually takes me home."

She winked. "Oh! Of course he does. *Duh, Mallory.* Okay, I'll pick you up around five instead?"

I nodded. "Sure, five will be fine."

"This is so exciting! I'll see you this afternoon, girlie!" She hugged me once more and then she was gone, leaving only a cloud of perfume.

———

AFTER SCHOOL, as I was walking toward Brayden's car, Derek ran into me, literally.

He stumbled backward and turned around, still laughing with his friends. When his eyes met mine, he fell silent. "Oh, hey, Jaicey." He rubbed his hand through his hair casually.

I smiled at him, looking at the pavement. "Hey, Derek."

"How, um—" He looked back toward his friends and then at me, before leaning down and speaking softly. "How are you?"

"I'm fine," I told him, kicking a rock around. *Walk away.*

He leaned down so that only I could hear his voice. "I know that you are his now, but I'm not giving up on us, okay? Five years isn't going to be lost because of what happened. I refuse to lose you like this." He gritted his teeth as the last sentence came out. I stared at him. God, he was gorgeous. Before I knew what was happening, his lips were on mine, his hands on my neck. *My neck.*

My body went into full panic. I tensed up, a scream tearing from my throat. I pulled away, my cheeks burning. "Derek!" I wiped my lips off. "What do you think you are doing? You can't just...kiss me like that. You have no right."

Before he could answer, I ran away, straight toward Brayden's car. Brayden was nowhere in sight. I turned around to look for him, and when I finally saw him, my heart dropped. He had seen everything and now he was walking toward Derek, fists clenched.

"Brayden," I called to him, waving my hand to catch his attention. It was no use. His eyes were locked on Derek, his jaw tight.

Derek, still watching me, saw that my line of vision was directed to just behind him. He turned around to see who I was waving at, just in time for Brayden's fist to make forceful contact with his face, and then again and again. Derek wasn't trying to fight back; he fell to the ground, limp.

"I'm sorry, man," he offered, holding his hands up in an attempt to cover his face. I waited for him to swing back, to push Brayden away, but he never did.

Brayden stomped his foot into Derek's stomach and leaned down to his face, though I could still hear every word he said. "If we weren't on school property, you can bet this would be a lot worse. You stay the hell away from her." Before he stood up, he leaned down once more and spit straight into Derek's face. Derek lay unmoving as Brayden strutted away, his face cold as stone.

I had never seen Brayden so mad. He didn't speak to me the whole way home. Once I did try to speak, but he turned up the radio, deterring any further attempts. What he had done to Derek was hard to watch and it was harsh, but I knew he did it to protect me. He had seen what Derek did and knew how much it had upset me. He was just doing what he thought I needed. I couldn't fault him for that.

What really bothered me was how Derek hadn't bothered to fight back. Derek was quite a bit bigger than Brayden, and it would have at least been an even fight, but he just stayed still. At the last second, as Brayden had been walking away, Derek looked at me with his bloodied eyes and I saw only hurt shining through them. I didn't see anger in his face at all. The complete opposite of Brayden. In that moment, his eyes were locked on mine with only sadness.

When we pulled up to my house, Brayden turned down the radio and I turned to him, willing him to look at me. "Are you okay? Are we going to talk about this at all?" I asked.

He grabbed hold of my wrist firmly, squeezing it until I let out a squeal. "I want you to stay away from him." He threw my arm back at me. I tried to pretend it hadn't hurt, rubbing my wrist gently as I climbed out of his car without a look back. I walked inside, feeling numb and trying not to look at the spot where I could still feel his fingerprints. I couldn't tell my parents. It would only upset them. Brayden was just mad, and he had every right to be, but this would never happen again.

I was lying on the couch, listening to Mom bustle around in the kitchen when I heard a knock on the door. I immediately jumped up, hoping it was Brayden. Instead, I saw wavy blonde hair and perfect teeth smiling at me.

Mallory. *Smile.* "Oh, hey, Mallory!" I had forgotten all about the plans we made.

"Hey, girl! You ready?" she asked, looking into the house behind me.

I just wasn't up for hanging out with anyone. "Oh, actually, I totally forgot but I have to—"

"Mallory?" I heard my mom's voice behind me.

"Mrs. Thomas! Oh my gosh, it's been so long! Oh, what have you done with your hair? You look so pretty." She beamed, pushing past me and gathering my mom into a familiar hug.

My mom looked positively warm inside, hugging her back. "Me? *Look at you.* I'm so glad to see you. I'd hoped you'd start coming back around. I know we've all missed seeing you. What are you girls planning tonight? Will you be staying for dinner?"

"Oh, I've missed you, too. I was so glad when Jaicey agreed to squeeze me into her busy schedule, what with the new boy and all." She gave me a sly look, wiggling her hips. "We were going to go out for dinner. Just to try and catch up, if that's all right?"

"Of course that's all right! That's just what Jaicey needs. Just remember, girls, it's a school night. Mallory, please tell your mom hello from me. I hope you all have a great time." She kissed my forehead and headed back to the kitchen, waving happily to us both.

"So, what were you going to say?" Mallory asked, her perfect smile still beaming.

"Nothing," I muttered, grinning smugly.

She turned to walk out the door, pointing to her car. "Okay, then. Let's go!"

CHAPTER TWENTY-THREE

When we arrived at Cecil's, the local hangout spot, Mallory led us to a booth. "Wow," she said, "feels like it's been forever, huh?"

I nodded, wringing my hands in my lap and praying I wasn't showing how awkward I felt. "Yeah, forever." *Literally, because we've never been here before.* Or wait...did I just not remember being here? The nightmare from the other night still haunted me. I couldn't be sure if it had been real.

A pretty, plump waitress came by our booth and took our orders. Mallory ordered a salad and a water. I ordered a burger and fries. She giggled at me. "Still haven't lost your appetite, I see. I always used to envy that about you." She looked down. I nodded. Everyone knew she was a recovering bulimic.

"So, how's Tyler doing?" I tried to fill the silence.

"Oh, you know, he's perfect. We've really been doing so great lately. I know we had some problems before—" *Yeah, like him hooking up with the entire rest of the cheer-*

leading squad, for example. "But we're really, really happy now. I really think I love him, Jaicey. Senior year has been so good to us. We've even been talking about getting a place together once we start college."

I nodded. "That's good, Mallory. I'm happy for you. Tyler's a really good guy," I lied to her. I didn't know Tyler at all, aside from the occasional jokes he cracked in Spanish class.

She smiled at me as our food arrived and we waited for the waitress to walk away. She stared at her salad for a few seconds before saying, like it was a confession, "I just, I really worry about what will happen to us once we go off to college next year if we don't go to the same one. He's talking about going to Penn State, but I'd really like to stay around here. I've even thought about going to stay with my sister in Charleston. We'll be so far apart, though, you know? I just don't know if we're ready for that. Living together seems like a good idea, right?"

I shook my head, swallowing a fry. "You guys will be fine, I'm sure. You've always been fine. Even after…" I trailed off, not sure where I was planning to go with that statement.

"Yeah." She seemed to know what I meant, even if I didn't. "I know." She reached up and squeezed my hand on top of the table. I tried so hard not to let her see me flinch. "I'm glad that you've found someone to make you happy, too, Jaice. I really, really am. I have to say, though, I really always thought you and Derek would be it. You guys were—"

I cleared my throat. She stopped, looking pained. "We were what?" I asked her.

115

"Nothing, never mind." She took a bite of her salad carefully.

"What were you going to say, Mallory? What were you going to say about me and Derek?" I demanded.

"What do you think I was going to say, Jaicey?"

"I don't know what you were going to say."

"Never mind." She looked down, nodding.

"Mallory?" I asked her, my voice testy. I was done dancing around this.

"Okay, Jaice, enough with the small talk. I mean, I feel like I'm walking on eggshells here. I don't know what I can say and what I can't. I don't want to upset you or break the rules. I just want my friend back. I just want to be able to talk to you, like we used to. This is all just so confusing."

I stared at her in disbelief. What did that even mean? She dropped her fork, covering her mouth. "Oh, look at me being selfish. Jaicey, I didn't mean that. Sometimes I don't think before I speak. My momma always says it's going to get me into trouble someday. Just ignore me. If it's confusing for me, I can't even imagine what this must be like for you."

She reached for my hand again but I kept it just out of her reach. Eventually, she pulled hers back and picked up her fork again. "The point is, we miss you. We all really, really miss you. We want to see you again, to hang out with you. We want it to go back to the way it was. I know after everything you've been through, that must be hard. God, I can't imagine what this must be like for you, but if you'll just talk to us, tell us what's going on inside of your mind, we'll try to help you. We want to help, but we can't when you keep pushing us all away. We're your friends, girl. We love you." She took a deep breath, begging me to say something.

I didn't know what to say. I just stared around at different parts of the room. Finally, deciding to speak, I tucked my hair behind my ear, trying to hide my panic and stood up. "Umm, I have to go to the bathroom."

She frowned as I stood up, walking out the door and to the nearest bus stop. When I looked back, she was staring at me through the glass, a look of sheer disappointment on her face. She didn't stand up, she didn't come after me, and she didn't try to stop me. Instead, she watched me leave, keeping her distance. A look of understanding filled her face.

CHAPTER TWENTY-FOUR

Brayden wasn't at school Wednesday or Thursday, and he wasn't returning my calls. Panic was starting to set in. I went to each class trying to act as though I wasn't worried, but my whole body was on edge. Where was he? Was he still mad? Why wouldn't he just talk to me?

I saw Derek in the hall a few times. He looked bad. His lips and eyes were still swollen. We avoided eye contact. Finally, on Friday, Brayden called. "Hey," he said casually as if he'd just spoken to me hours ago.

"Hey? *Really?* What is going on, Brayden? Where are you? I haven't heard from you in three days, you haven't called, and you haven't shown up at school. Do you have any idea how worried I've been about you? I didn't know what was happening, what I was supposed to do. And then you just call and say hey? Like nothing happened? Like we're fine. Are we fine?"

"Look, I'm sorry, Jaice. I was just stressed out, okay? I had to blow off some steam."

"And you do that by disappearing? By ignoring me? You could've at least let me know that you were okay."

"I know, I know." He still sounded angry. "Look, do you want to hang out with me or would you rather just keep being pissed off?"

I stopped, biting my lip. "I'm not—"

"You are."

"Fine, I am. I just missed you. I'm sorry. I was just so worried."

He sighed. "I know. I'm sorry, too. It was just, seeing him kiss you drove me insane. You're my girl, Jaicey Thomas. Mine. I don't ever want to see you with anyone else. I don't know what I'd do."

"You're right. I'm *your* girl. Yours and only yours, and no matter what anyone does, nothing will ever change that. Do you hear me?"

"Promise me?"

"I promise."

"So, let's hang out."

BRAYDEN WAS at my house nearly fifteen minutes after we hung up. I opened the door and dragged him inside. "Come on! Come on!"

He followed me to the bedroom. "What are we doing?"

"I have to show you my dress," I shouted proudly, running past Mom and Dad.

"Hey, Brayden." They waved as we shot through the house.

He waved happily to them. When we entered my

room, I shot straight for my closet and he sat down on the bed. I grabbed hold of the hanger, excitement filling me. "Dum-da-da-dum," I announced as I twirled around in circles with it, the red fabric swirling around my legs. He smiled.

"Well? What do you think?" I asked when he didn't say anything.

"I think you're beautiful." He stood, pulling me to him and kissing me square on the lips.

"Well, thanks." I smiled at him, heat rushing to my face. "But I was actually showing you the dress."

He let go of me. "Oh, I hadn't even noticed that." He stared down at it. "Well, it's beautiful, too."

I studied his eyes, trying to decide where his head had been. "God, I've missed you so much."

"I've missed you, too," he said, pressing his lips to mine. He took the dress from me and hung it up carefully. Then, he grabbed my hand and led me to the bed.

"Are you ready for tomorrow night?" I asked.

"Of course I am. I have such a night planned for us, you wouldn't believe it."

"Oh, you do?" I asked, my eyebrows raised.

He kissed me. "I do."

"I can't wait." He held my hand, kissing each of my fingers tenderly.

"Promise me something?" I asked.

"Anything," he swore, still kissing my hand.

"Whatever has been going on, no matter what it is from here on out, please don't block me out like this. Please. Just talk to me. No matter what it is, I'm here. I can handle it. I need you to stay with me, no matter what."

He pulled me to his side, wrapping his arm around my neck. "I promise, Jaice. I told you I'm sorry. It's just that I told you about my mom, and with my dad working all the time, well, I've never really had someone care about me. I've never had anyone to answer to."

I hugged him back. "Well, I'm here now. You have me, and I care. I care a lot."

He kissed the side of my head, my pulse quickening, this time in a good way. "I love you."

"I love you, too." He pulled away, staring at me, shock on his face. "I mean it; I've been thinking about it nonstop lately. I love you, Brayden. I love you so much," I admitted.

His face fell flat, warmth filling his eyes. "I told you I'd wait," he whispered in my ear as he hugged me tight. He pulled me into a kiss, our lips meeting with a passion we'd never had before. My cheeks burned, blushing. We lay down on the bed, his hands cradling my head. I kissed him like I'd never kissed anyone. *Or like I never remember kissing anyone.* My body turned frigid. I flinched under his touch for the first time in ages. He let me go, sitting up.

"Brayden, I—" I tried to apologize, but there was nothing to be said. Words failed me.

"It's fine, Jaicey," he said, I hoped that he meant it. He stood up, turning toward the door.

"Please don't go. I'm sorry. It's just instinct."

"Why? Why is it instinct?" He spun, his hands in the air. "Why is it not okay for me to disappear for a few days but it's fine for you to flinch every time I touch you?" I looked at the hurt in his face, begging me for answers I didn't know myself.

"Someone hurt you," he said. It wasn't a question, but I

nodded anyway. "Who?" He walked closer to me, his arms ready to hold me.

I paused, thinking long and hard. What answer could he handle? What answer could I give?

"Who hurt you, Jaicey?" he asked, his voice growing firm. He grasped my arms, not in a painful way, but enough to make me flinch again. "For God's sake, Jaicey, tell me."

"I don't...I don't know," I said, trying to keep my voice under control.

He dropped my arms. "You don't know?"

I shook my head, rubbing my arms where his hands had been. "No."

"What do you mean you don't know?"

"I just don't know." I wished I could tell him more, wished I had more to tell. Instead, I stared at him solemnly, waiting for his response.

He turned back for the door. "Fine. Whatever."

"Brayden, please. I want to tell you, I do. I just...I don't know. Please. Please don't leave. Not like this."

"Like what?" He stared at me.

"Angry. Mad. Whatever you are."

"I'm not angry, Jaicey. I'm not mad. I'm hurt. I'm hurt that you don't trust me, but it's fine. It's whatever."

"It's not fine. I know that. I'm sorry." He waited for me to elaborate but I didn't. After a moment, he grasped the door handle. "Please don't leave while we're fighting," I begged, feeling tears form in my eyes.

"We aren't fighting, Jaice." He stared at me sadly.

"We aren't?" I asked. He shook his head. "Then, where are you going?"

"Away." He kissed my head quickly. "Now it's your turn to wait."

"I love you," I called after him, wishing he'd come back but he was already out the door.

"I love you, too," he replied. Just as quickly as he'd come, he was gone.

CHAPTER TWENTY-FIVE

The next day was pure chaos. I shot out of bed at 4:04, as always. This time, however, I was grateful for the early start. I hopped in the shower, letting the warm water and steam steady my nerves. I had never been so excited and nervous all at once. I ran a bath and let myself soak until I heard my mother in the kitchen at six.

After breakfast, we headed to the salon, where my mom paid seventy-five dollars to have someone pull and prod every inch of my head until my hair looked, in her words, 'fabulous!' At the end of the appointment, the stylist attempted to turn me around for what she called 'the big reveal.' Mom grabbed my chair seconds before I'd seen the mirror and shouted, "Sorry, we're in a hurry. She looks great." She paid while I, still shaking, waited in the car.

By the end of the day, my hair had been done, my nails had been painted, makeup had been layered on my face, and I had about a gallon of perfume on. As I slipped the dress over my head, my mom came into the room.

"You almost ready, honey?" she asked, sticking her head through the doorway. She gasped when she saw me, tears instantly filling her eyes. "Oh, Jaicey."

"Do I look okay?" I asked, knowing the answer by the look on her face.

"Oh, sweetheart. You look beautiful." She smiled at me, twirling a strand of my hair around her finger and letting it bounce back into place beside my face. I turned around, holding my hair up to allow her to zip the dress. She did. "I'm going to go ahead back downstairs and get the camera. Give me a minute to make it down before you start coming."

I nodded. She patted me on the cheek once, covering her mouth with one hand, tears still framing her eyes, and then she walked out of the room. I twirled around my room, feeling as if I were five years old and dressed up as a princess again. I ran my hands down my hips, trying to imagine what I must look like, trying to draw out my time until I descended the stairs. Finally, the clock struck eight o'clock. It was still too early for Brayden to have arrived, but I could think of nothing else to do. I picked up my heels and began to carry them down the stairs.

Mom had the camera ready as soon as I came out of my room. "You look beautiful, honey. Doesn't she look great, Chuck?" she cried, snapping pictures. My dad stood up from his chair, his mouth agape as he watched me walk toward him.

"You look amazing, sweetheart," he said finally, agreeing with my mom. As I reached the bottom of the stairs and stood in front of him, he held his arms out and took me into them. He wrapped his arms around me, hugging me tightly as I heard Mom snapping pictures.

"All right, now pretend like you're dancing with her, Chuck," she instructed.

Dad and I posed as we were directed. He kissed me on the forehead, and Mom took one more snapshot. We both smiled at each other sadly, knowing we would never see these pictures. There wasn't a single picture more recent than my fifteenth birthday in the entire house. It was like we'd just stopped existing, like life had stopped altogether. In a way, I guess it had.

Once the picture-taking stopped, I sat down in Dad's chair and pulled up the bottom of my dress slightly, offering up my shoes. "Pretty please?" I asked.

Dad laughed. "As you wish, princess." He bent down to help me buckle my shoes. Mom snapped another picture.

"So are you nervous, Jaice?" she asked.

"A little bit, yeah," I admitted. "Mostly just excited though."

"It'll be fine, I promise. You guys will have so much fun. You'll never want it to end. Prom is just so magical. Did I ever tell you it was at our prom that I decided I was going to marry your father?"

"No." I shook my head. "You never told me that."

"You never even told me that," my dad joked, standing up. He chortled under his breath.

"It sure was. It really is a special night." She nodded, a distant smile on her face.

"Well, I don't think we're quite there yet, but I still think we'll have a lot of fun," I said.

Dad was still laughing. I looked over at him. "You okay over there, Dad?" I asked, but it was obvious he wasn't okay. His laughter had turned into more of a choking fit, his face turning a deep shade of purple, and he was making a weird sort of clicking noise with his tongue. A seizure. He fell to the ground, thudding as he landed.

My mom immediately went into action, grabbing my dad and turning him on his side so that he wouldn't choke on his tongue. "Chuck! It's okay, it's okay." She was using the same soothing voice that she had so often used with me when I was growing up.

"Do I need to call nine-one-one?" I asked, snapping back into action.

He stopped shaking, stiff as a board. She shook her head, starting to lift him into a standing position. He was still out of it. "No. We'll just have to take him to the ER anyway." She looked me up and down, realization setting in on her face. "Jaicey, I'm so sorry."

"No, no, there'll be other dances, other dates. Brayden will understand."

She walked him out to the car and got him buckled in while I was grabbing my jacket and cell phone, trying to find Brayden's number. My hands were shaking. I was inconsolable. She met me at the door, her hand held up in protest, shaking her head fiercely. "No. This is your night, Jaice. Your father would never forgive himself if you missed it. You stay. We'll be home as soon as possible. Have fun, sweetheart, and be safe. We love you. You look beautiful." She kissed my cheek, running her fingers over my hair one last time.

"No, Mom, please. I want to go with you."

"No, Jaicey. This isn't a negotiation. You are going to prom. The doctor will take a look at your dad and send us straight home. You would have missed this night all for nothing. I won't allow it. You stay. Have fun." She shut the door, and just like that, she was gone.

CHAPTER TWENTY-SIX

It was nearly nine o'clock and I was a mess. "Mom, please call me. I need to know what's going on," I shouted into my phone. "It's been almost an hour and you aren't answering your phone. Should I be worried? I just, I need to know. Please call me." I hung up the phone after leaving my second voicemail, and my strength finally shattered. The tears that had been building up in my eyes were now pouring down my face, ruining all of my makeup. I was a cliché; crying on prom night, and the worst part was I hadn't even made it to prom yet.

Nothing about the night was right. This was supposed to be my special night, and it had started out as a big catastrophe. I wasn't in the mood to dance anymore, and I wasn't in the mood to have fun. I just wanted more than anything to be there with my mom and dad as they talked to the doctor. It wasn't right for me to be here, waiting to go have the time of my life while my dad was lying on a cold table, having tests run on him in a smelly hospital. None of this was right.

That was all it took. I stood up, grabbing my cell phone and finding Brayden's number. I threw my jacket hastily over my shoulders as his line began ringing. I swung the door open and let out a scream. There was Brayden, standing in my doorway, arm up, ready to knock. I put the phone down. My jaw dropped.

"Oh, Brayden. Hi," I mumbled, wiping off my face and blinking quickly in an attempt to dry my eyes.

Without hesitation he cradled my cheeks, pushing me into the living room. "Jaicey, what's wrong?" he asked with urgency. "What happened? You weren't about to bail on me, were you?"

Something about him was off that night. I should've noticed it immediately, but with everything going on inside my head, I just didn't. I sniffed. "I'm okay. It's just my dad."

"Your dad?" he asked.

"Yes. I haven't told you yet. I haven't told anyone. But he's...my dad is sick. He's really, really sick and I need to go see him right now. He needs me. I'm sorry. I know it's the worst possible timing, but I just need to be with him. This doesn't feel right."

Despite what I had said, he didn't move out of the way to let me leave or offer me a ride. Instead, he shut the door and gently pushed me backward. "Whoa, whoa, calm down, Jaice. It's okay. Just breathe for me, okay? Slow down. Let's talk about this some more before you decide anything."

I didn't bother resisting. Instead, I let him sit me down on the couch. I took a deep breath as he began rubbing my back patiently. "Now, calm down. Let's start from the beginning, okay? Slowly. Tell me what's going on."

I slowed down, tears still streaming down my cheeks. "A few weeks ago, the day you found me at the hospital, my dad was diagnosed with a stage two brain tumor. It's inoperable. He has seizures because of it. He just had one, and my mom had to rush him to the hospital. It may be nothing; Mom says it probably is and I'm probably just overreacting but it was terrifying. Seeing him like that was the scariest thing I've ever seen. I just really want to be sure that he's okay—Brayden, what are you doing?"

He was leaning in closer to me, just inches between us now. He kissed my cheekbone. "Go on."

"Okay. He's okay, I think, but what if he's not, you know? What if he's really not okay and he needs me? What if my mom needs me and I'm not there because I'm here and—hey, stop!" His kisses trailed down my collar, onto my neck. He stopped my protest by kissing me firmly on the lips. I pushed him back. "Brayden, stop it. I'm trying to talk to you."

"You look beautiful tonight. Have I told you that?" He continued kissing my face, my nose, my forehead. He lowered his lips to my jaw line. I moved back until I reached the arm of the couch and could pull back no further. He had me pinned.

"No, but thank you. I really need to leave now. I can catch the bus if you want to head over to the school."

"You want me to go alone? Like a loser? As if no one wanted to go with me?"

I furrowed my brow, so confused by what was

happening. *"What?* No. I just really need to leave. I'm so, so sorry."

"No, Jaicey. You can't do this to me. I love you, remember? Stay with me, please. Stay here," he begged, like a child.

"Brayden." His kisses had worked their way down to my collar bone again. "I really am sorry. You know what? Why don't you go ahead and go and I'll call you when I leave the hospital and then we can arrive together. Fashionably late, right?" I laughed nervously, my checks flaming.

He kissed my neck, his lips brushing my scars. I instinctively covered them with my hand. He pulled it down forcefully. "You don't have to be embarrassed by your scars, Jaice. I love them so much."

"What did you say?" I pushed him back. He'd never mentioned my scars before, never even looked at them from what I'd seen. It was part of the reason I'd liked him so much. Why I'd loved him.

"Your scars." He smiled. His eyes had a menacing look to them I hadn't noticed before. "Everyone has them. Want to see mine?" His smile grew threatening. He sat up, keeping one hand on my stomach so that I stayed pinned down. He then proceeded to slide his jacket off, never letting me up. He unbuttoned the white shirt underneath slowly, never breaking eye contact with me. He turned around. "Look at my scratches, Jaicey. See my scar? What do you think?" I laid eyes on a solid red line running from his mid-back up over his right shoulder. I flinched, though he'd made no move toward me. I knew where that scar had come from. My heart pounded, my throat going dry. Every part of my body grew cold. My hair stood on end. My organs felt as though they had turned to solid ice. I couldn't move, couldn't scream.

I tried to stand up but he swung his arm around, stopping me. There was nothing I could do, nowhere I could go. I looked at the door and then at him. How had I never noticed the savage in his eyes? Without thinking, I rolled off the couch, sinking to the floor and crawling under the glass coffee table.

CRASH. His fist went through the glass, blood splattering me. He grabbed my hair through the table and pulled me up, the shards cutting my arms and shoulders as I went through the broken top. He flung me onto the floor with all of his might, and I heard my wrist crack as I landed. The pain shot through me like lightning. I cried out, my scream horrific.

He grabbed my broken wrist, pushing on it until I screamed again. I kicked him with my heel, crawling across the floor and ignoring the excruciating pain. He was too quick. I bolted for the door, but before I knew what was happening, he stood above me, smiling down. I tried to shove him, but he twisted my arm.

It hit me then that this was his plan all along. He was going to win. My wrist throbbed and my head spun as everything happened too fast. If I could only make it to the kitchen, there was a drawer with knives that I could grab. I put my good arm behind me, trying to scoot away, but I didn't budge. He didn't say anything, just watched me try. In one final attempt, I put my foot firmly on the ground, pushing myself back. *Riiiip.*

I looked down, staring at where my dress should have

been. The bottom had completely detached, still stuck to the floor under his shoe. This was my chance. I knew I should run, but I couldn't move. I stared at my legs, pale from lack of sunlight. I gasped as I saw it, a thin red scar running from my upper thigh around to the back of my knee; a scar like Brayden's. Seeing the scar made me dizzy and then I remembered.

I remembered everything.

CHAPTER TWENTY-SEVEN

I
t was the night of Dan Murphy's party. The last day of my
freshman year. Everyone who was, or wanted to be, anyone
was there. I had told my parents that I was staying with Bailey
and she had told her mom that we were staying with Mallory's
sister in college. By the time we had all arrived to the party,
most of the people there were already drunk. A group of senior
guys had started throwing people into the pool. I remembered
the way Derek had pulled me close when any of the boys had
gotten close, though we knew they weren't noticing me. We were
still freshmen, practically babies in their eyes. At some point
that night, I had lost sight of Mallory and Tyler, though I
couldn't be sure of exactly when. Bailey had also been lost at
some point throughout the night. I remembered that the house
smelled like cigarette smoke and vomit, but I tried to pretend it
didn't bother me. It was our anniversary, Derek and I. We'd
been elementary school sweethearts, joined at the hip, insepara-
ble. While he had wanted to take me out to dinner, I had
insisted that we go to Dan's party.

After we got in that night and settled, I had excused myself to go to the restroom. Dan's mother had more perfume than I'd ever seen and I took time smelling each and every one, dabbing them delicately on my wrist. When I finally found the one I liked, I dabbed it on my neck. I remember looking at myself in the mirror, seeing the way my long, red hair cascaded down my slender, unscarred neck. I noticed the way my bright silver eyes shone a little extra when I smiled and the way my teeth were naturally white. I was pretty, and there was something about that night that had made me glow even more.

When I walked out of the bathroom and went to look for Derek, I found him standing with a bunch of his friends around the pool table. They were laughing. I remember catching a glimpse of Mallory sitting with Tyler and a group of juniors, fitting right in. We were all way out of our league and we knew it, but Mal and I weren't going to let it be that way. We refused to settle for less than what we wanted.

The party got pretty wild, I even heard rumors that it ended up getting broken up by the police. Of course, I wasn't around to find out.

After a few hours at the party, Derek brought me into a quiet room. We'd both already had a lot to drink. No—maybe it was just me that had been drinking. "Can we please go?" he asked, holding my hand.

"Derek, no. I thought you wanted to be here. You agreed. Don't you want to start summer out the right way?"

"Of course I do."

"Okay then, being here is the only way to make sure that we do that," I insisted.

"And I've been here, Jaicey. I'm here. But this isn't how I want our anniversary to be. I want it to be me and you."

"This is where all of the cool kids are, Derek. If we want to be popular, this is where we need to be. We can't leave early."

"I don't honestly care if I look cool or not. What I care about is having you with me. There will be plenty of parties, ones with our friends. People we actually know."

"Do you care about making me happy at all?" I screamed at him, the alcohol making my head spin.

"Of course I do!"

"If you really do—" I shouted at him, dropping his hand dramatically. "If you really care about me at all, you should understand why this is important to me. Because it is, Derek. This party, being surrounded by these people, this is it. This is what high school's all about."

"It doesn't have to about this, Jaicey. Surrounded by people we don't even know, being too drunk to remember anything. Why can't we just go? It's our anniversary. There'll be other parties. There'll be other nights."

"Why can't you ever just let me have any fun? It's one night, Derek. I am so sick of you taking me to movies by ourselves, and picnics by ourselves. I want to hang out with other people... and I can do that with or without you. If you can't accept that, then you can just leave."

I hadn't mean to say it, of course. I was just upset. In the end, that didn't matter. I didn't get to tell him that, or that I was sorry, which I was. That was the last time I saw him that night. That was the last thing I said to him.

I stormed out of the bedroom, tunneling through the crowd, ignoring Derek as he called my name. When I got outside, he was there. Waiting for me.

Looking back, I guess I should have been surprised, but at the time my anger surpassed my confusion. When I saw him, he *called me over. I ran straight up to him, crying over the fight. I had always talked to him about my problems; I didn't for a second think that that night would be any different. Boy, was I wrong.*

Mr. Brown was one of my best friends, even though he was a teacher. He was cool. He was always the first person to say hello to me in the mornings, the first person to tell me I looked pretty when I felt like I was having a bad hair day. He told me that I was smart, that I was special, that I had a bright future, and so, I believed him. I told him when my parents considered divorce. I talked to him about what I wanted to do after high school. When my grandfather passed away, when Bailey and I were fighting—whatever the problem—it was Mr. Brown who had comforted me.

Bailey. Oh God, Bailey. B. Her name struck me deep into my chest. Bailey was my best friend, as much as I had wanted to forget that, as much as I had tried to forget her.

It was Bailey who had drawn the picture of me hanging on my bedroom wall. She was going to be an artist. We were going to tour Spain together after graduation. We had it all planned out. That one night changed everything.

"What's wrong, sweetie?" Mr. Brown asked, pushing his glasses further up onto his nose.

"What are you doing here?" I asked him, my voice slurring partially from the alcohol, partially from my tears.

"I heard you talking about this party today in class. I came to make sure you were okay. I would never ever tell your parents, of course, but I needed to make sure that you were staying out of trouble. Here, give me your cell phone and I'll put my number in it, so you can call me in case you need anything tonight."

"Mr. Brown, you already gave me your number, remember? I have it."

"Oh, right. Well, I forgot to tell you I got a new number, so it's different now. Come on, give me your phone." He held out his hand, waiting.

Without thinking I handed him my phone, hoping he wouldn't smell the alcohol on my breath. I watched as he began pressing buttons.

A voice interrupted us. "Jaicey? Is that you? Thank God, I've been looking all over for you. Derek is frantic. Hey, what are you doing over there? Who are you talking to?"

"It's Mr. Brown, B. Come here."

I heard her footsteps getting closer. "Jaice, Derek is freaking out looking for you. What happened?"

"We just had a fight, Bailey. It's fine. No big deal."

"Maybe we should go back inside." It was Bailey who had been suspicious, I could see it in the way she looked at me, but I wouldn't hear of it. Bailey was always the cautious to my extreme. She was tame when I was wild. She was calm when I'd gone mad. I thought she was just being childish, uncool even. What I wouldn't give now to have listened to her, to have trusted her.

"No. I need to clear my head. It's fine, Bailey. Go inside if you want to."

"No," she said. I felt her lock her pinky around mine, our sign of safety.

"She's right, Jaicey. You girls go on back inside. I'll see you at school."

"Oh, okay," I said, sad to see him leaving.

He walked back to his car, stopping to turn around. "Oh, Jaicey?"

"Yeah?" I called out.

"Don't forget to call me if you need anything. I put my new number in your phone."

I nodded. "I will. Thank you for coming to check on me, Mr. Brown." He continued to walk away, staring at me intently. "Oh, wait, Mr. Brown," I called out to him, tapping my pockets.

"Yes?"

"You still have my phone! Hang on just a second."

He stopped by his passenger's door and reached into his pocket, pulling out my phone and pointing at it, a goofy grin on his face. "Oh, look at that. Silly me, you're right."

I ran up to his car, hearing Bailey's footsteps following close behind me. I reached for my phone.

"Wait a second, don't I get a hug?" He held out his arms.

Without hesitation, I leaned in and wrapped my arms around his pudgy stomach. "Thank you so much for everything."

"Come on, Jaicey. Derek is going to be worried," Bailey called from behind me.

Mr. Brown wrapped his arms around me and for a second we just stood there. Then, before I realized what was happening, he was shoving me into his car. I was so confused. It never even occurred to me that I should scream, not even when I felt Bailey's weight land on top of me. She, on the other hand, was fully prepared to scream and that's exactly what she did. Her screaming brought me back to reality and I began screaming as loud as I could. We locked pinkies, screaming as he made his way around to the driver's door. It was no use. No one could hear us over the blaring music, and no one had seen us. Mr. Brown wasn't taking any chances regardless. I'm not sure what *he hit her with, but when I felt her head slam into mine, it all went black.*

———

WHEN I HAZILY OPENED MY *eyes what seemed like years later, I heard water splashing all around me, as if we were on a boat. I tried to sit up, but my head felt as though it weighed a thousand pounds.*

I lay back down, groaning and rubbing my head, trying to figure out where I was.

I heard her voice echo across the dark room. "Jaicey? Is that you? Are you awake?" she whispered.

"Bailey?" I called out to her, my head pounding.

"Shhh! He'll hear you," she said quickly.

"Who will?" I asked, my voice still loud.

"Jaicey, whisper! If he hears us, he'll come back. You have to be quiet. He keeps checking on us, but I think we're safe as long as he thinks were still asleep."

For a second, I had no idea what she was talking about, but then my memory came back to me. She seemed far away from me, though I couldn't be sure. The room was pitch black and cold.

I whispered to her, my voice shaky. "Bailey, where are we?"

"I, I don't know, exactly. It seems like some sort of basement. I think we're beside the lake. Do you hear the water? It reminds me of being on Daddy's houseboat. We aren't moving though. We have to be on the shore."

"I don't understand what is happening. I mean, it's Mr. Brown. He was my friend."

"Tell me about it." She sighed. "I'm really scared."

"How long have you been awake?"

"I don't know, Jaice. A day, maybe? I've tried to stay awake, but I keep falling back asleep. At least a day, maybe more."

"A day? How long have we been here?"

"I don't know," she whispered, her voice sounding small.

"Bailey, why hasn't anyone come for us? Surely they know we're missing."

I heard her sob. "They think we're in Charleston for the weekend, remember? We weren't even supposed to be back until Monday. They might not even know we're gone."

"They know, Bailey. Surely they know. Derek would've told them, right? Surely he would've told them." We both knew I was lying, though she didn't argue with me. No one knew where we were, and no one knew we were missing.

"Are you tied up, too?" she asked.

"Yeah," I replied.

"I keep trying to wiggle out, but it just hurts so badly. He's got it tied so tight."

"What do you think he wants, Bailey?" I asked the question neither of us truly wanted to answer.

"I don't know."

"I can't believe this. He was always so nice."

She didn't answer. Bailey had never liked Mr. Brown, had never trusted him like I had. She thought our friendship was weird. "I'm sorry, Bailey. I'm so sorry. This is all my fault."

"It's okay, Jaicey. You couldn't have known."

I sobbed loudly, forgetting I should be quiet. "Of course I could've known. You warned me about him."

"Jaicey, shhh!" she begged.

It was too late. We heard the heavy footsteps up above us immediately. I squeezed my hands into fists, wriggling to get *free, but it was no use. A door crept open and a bright light shone into my eyes, burning them fiercely. He entered the room and shut the door behind him, leaving us in the dark once again.*

I heard his voice through the darkness, filled with venom. "Hello, ladies. Finally awake, I hear."

Neither of us answered. "Not going to answer me?"

Silence still. If we were quiet enough, maybe he wouldn't be able to find us. I felt his warm breath on my face suddenly, felt his boot crunch down on my fingers. I let out a painful cry as I felt the bones in my hand snap.

"Jaicey!" Bailey cried out. "Leave her alone!"

He took his foot off of my hand. "Oh, so you are awake, then? I just wanted to make sure."

I couldn't hold it in any longer. Confusion spilled out of me in the form of tears. "You were my friend. How can you do this to me? I trusted you. I trusted you and you lied to me. How? Why?"

"Yes, yes, you're right," he said spitefully. "See, I had you pegged right from the beginning. So sweet, so trusting." His breath was back on my face, reeking of rotten milk and alcohol. "So pretty." He rubbed a piece of my hair gently. "And, of course, it helped that half of the money in the bank has your last name on it. I just had to come up with a plan. A plan that would allow me to become...what was it you called me? Oh yes, your friend." He said in a mocking tone. "I had to get close to you, Jaicey. I had to learn your weaknesses, to convince you that you could trust me. You made that all too easy. And then, the fact that you came in a two-pack." His breath left me and I heard him stride away. Bailey screamed out in pain. "Well, that was just a bonus."

I screamed, pushing myself up to leap at him but was torn back down by my ties. "You had this planned? All along? How could you? You're crazy!" I screamed, my voice feral.

Bailey's screams turned to whimpers, and I heard his foot-steps again. "You're probably right. I am crazy, but maybe I'm just crazy enough to make this work. Now, let's just get a few things straight. I don't want to hurt you girls, but that doesn't mean I won't. If your parents cooperate, you'll be set free, and you'll never hear from me again. However, if they don't, this room will be the last place you'll ever see. I do hope you've said goodbye to dear old Derek." He cackled loudly.

Hate soared through my body, my blood boiling. After a few moments, I heard his footsteps and saw the light of the door that told me he'd left the room. I waited until I could no longer hear him walking.

"You okay?"

There was a moment of quiet before she answered. "I'm okay. Are you?"

I tried to move my fingers; three of them wouldn't budge. My whole hand throbbed. "I'm okay," I confirmed, because even if I wasn't, what could be done?

We were silent for a few moments before I heard her voice again. "Jaicey?"

"Yeah?"

"Do you believe him? About letting us go?"

I didn't want to answer. Deep down, I knew the truth. "Of course," I lied to her. "Of course he'll let us go. He's not a killer, Bailey. He's just a mean old man who wants our parents' money. Once he has that, he'll disappear, just like he said."

She didn't answer.

"You have to believe that, okay, Bailey?"

She let out a heartbreaking sob. "I just want to go home."

I wanted more than anything to touch my best friend's hands, to tell her that everything would be okay, but with my hands tied and my hope deflated, I instead sat in silence, listening to our captor moving around up above.

THREE DAYS WENT *by before we saw Mr. Brown again. Three days of eating nothing and seeing no one. We sat in near-silence, both in and out of sleep. When the door crept open, the light brought physical pain to my eyes.*

"Get up!" he yelled. "God, you guys reek. You've really stunk the place up."

I sat up as carefully as I could, my arms still restrained to the ground below me. He flicked on a light. I cowered, attempting to hide my eyes. The room he had us in was small, about the size of a classroom, and bare. The walls were concrete, and I knew Bailey must've been right. We were in a basement of some sort. There was a chair in the middle of the room and ties on the walls like the ones binding Bailey and I down. Had he had other kids down here? Other girls like us? I looked at Bailey then, ready to cry when I saw her. Her eyes were bloodshot, her face pale. Her hand was black and blue, probably from where he'd smashed it. Her beautiful black hair was frazzled and muddy, and her clothes were soiled. We stared at each other for just a moment. She looked exhausted. Dying. The word hit me hard. She looked like she was dying. Were we dying?

Staring at Mr. Brown in the light made this all the more real. No longer could I pretend this was a nightmare and wait to wake up. This was happening. This was real. He held a phone in his hand, his fingers over the speaker.

"You have a phone call," he said cheekily.

"Who is it?"

"It's your dear old mommy." My heart leapt with hope. It was Mom. She'd know what to do.

He pulled a knife from his back pocket, wiggling it in the air. "One word about me or about where we are, and Bailey dies. Do you hear me?"

Bailey's eyes filled with tears as she began sobbing silently.

"I hear you." I nodded, never looking away from the knife.

I took the phone from his hand, my fingers numb, and placed it to my ear. I watched as he walked to Bailey, placing the knife on her neck and waiting for me to make a move.

"Mom?" I said into the phone, my voice feeling funny in my throat.

Sobs. Sobs rang out on the other line. I heard her trying to catch her breath."Jaicey, oh Jaicey, thank God. Jaicey, are you hurt? Are you okay? It's so good to hear your voice. Did he hurt you? Oh God."

My voice kept getting caught in my dry throat. "I'm okay, Mom. I'm okay. We're okay. We just want to come home."

"I know, sweetheart," she said through her sobs. "I know. I'm so sorry this happened. We're getting the money together today. Oh, Jaice, it's so good to hear your voice. You've been so brave, sweetheart. So, so brave. We love you so much, you know that?"

"I love you."

"Please stay safe, Jaicey. Please hold on. We're coming for you, okay? We're coming."

"Okay, Momma."

"Do you know who he is, Jaicey? Can you tell me who he is?"

My eyes darted to Bailey, the knife making a white line on her neck from pressure.

"No, Mom. I don't know."

She let out another sob. "I love you, Jaice. Please just hang in there."

Before I could say anything else, he leapt up and grabbed the phone from my hand, smashing it under his foot. I flinched, expecting him to do more. Instead, he picked up the pieces and strode from the room, turning the light out once more.

———

AFTER TWO MORE DAYS, *I awoke to Bailey coughing. I knew neither of us would make it much longer. Death didn't seem so scary anymore, honestly. It was almost comforting to know it would be over soon. It had become harder for me to stay awake for very long periods of time, and my mouth was always so dry. The smell of the room after the first day had made me sick, but now I didn't even notice it anymore.*

That day, I heard her voice for the first time in so long. "Jaicey?" It sounded hard for her to talk, her voice was gravelly like she'd been sleeping for a long time.

It took me forever to answer, trying to summon my voice from deep inside my throat. "Yeah?" I croaked.

"I don't feel much anymore. I think...I think I'm dying. Is this how it feels?"

"No...we're not...dying. Our parents are...coming for us. We're going to be...okay, Bailey."

"No," she said, and then there was more coughing.

It was hard for me to talk. Each sentence left me winded. "Yes, yes we are. You have to...believe that. You have to believe

147

that or...he wins. He can't keep us much longer. Do you know... how many people must be looking for us? My mom...said they were sending the money. That...means he'll have to...let us go." I had to fight to keep pushing my voice out and even then it sounded weird.

"You think so? Really?" She wasn't crying anymore; I don't think either of us really saw a point. Besides that, I didn't think my body had any extra water to release.

"I know so, and so does he," I said, though I wished I believed it.

She coughed again, with what little strength she had left in her. "I don't blame you, you know."

Relief flooded me at her words. "You don't?"

"Of course I don't. I didn't have to come with you. No one forced me. You're my best friend, Jaicey. I wouldn't want you to be here alone. Wherever here is."

I smiled, there was so much more that I wanted to say to her, so much I wanted to tell her before we were both gone, but I couldn't fight off sleep any longer.

THE NEXT TIME I was woken up, someone was touching me. "Bailey?" I asked. Had she gotten free?

The person didn't answer.

"What are you doing?" I asked, knowing immediately that those hands weren't Bailey's.

Still no answer. The hands were untying me. I stayed quiet, just knowing we were getting out. He untied my feet first. I felt his crisp mustache on my ear, smelled his coffee breath. "It's time," he whispered.

"I'm getting out? Going home?" I asked, feeling him untie my arms.

He grabbed hold of my arms forcefully, pulling me to sit up. "Not exactly." He let go of me, and I heard him walk away. I attempted to stand, though my legs were weak from lack of use. Before I could get up completely, a set of hands were on me and I was jerked back onto the floor. My head smacked the concrete and I landed in a puddle of some wet and warm liquid. Vomit rose in my throat.

"What's going on? Please! You said you'd let us go."

No voice answered but I felt steady, silent breathing on the back of my neck. Strong arms wrapped around my neck and shoulders. I didn't know what was happening, but I knew it wasn't over. I felt his hands unbuttoning my pants and sliding them down and I knew what would come next. I closed my eyes, unable to move, and tried to focus on my breathing. His hands were rough on the smooth skin of my legs, and I felt the vomit rising higher and higher in my throat.

I heard a moan from Bailey. For a moment, I'd forgotten she was in the room. "Bailey!" I shouted out. A fist slammed into my jaw and I tasted blood immediately.

"Go shut her up," I heard Mr. Brown whisper, still down near my legs. The hands around my shoulders released and for a second, I felt free. Then Mr. Brown's weight was on top of me. His knees were digging into my stomach. I vomited and then choked on the bile as it filled my mouth, unable to turn over. He turned me over, pounding on my back with a force I was sure would leave bruises. Not that anyone would ever find my body, I reminded myself. When he flipped me back over, I lay still on the concrete, now covered in vomit and whatever else I was laying in.

He moved his way back down to my feet and I knew if I was going to get out, now was the time. I kicked both of my feet at the same time with every ounce of power I had and heard Mr. Brown grunt. I had made contact. With any luck, I knew that would buy me a few seconds. I jumped up, but was immediately hit in the head with something else. I fell back down to my knees, tasting blood in my mouth once more. My nose began to bleed. This is it, *I thought.* This is when I die. *I knew I had only a few more moments of consciousness left. I was exhausted and my body screamed at me in pain. I had no idea where Bailey was, if she was even alive at all, and for all I knew, I was never getting out of this basement alive.*

"You said you'd let us go," I cried. "You promised." My last piece of hope.

"You promised," he mocked in a girly voice, laughing. "Did you honestly think that once I had my money I'd let you go to run off and tell the police what I've done? My darling, I thought you were smarter than that. You've seen my face. You know my name. Do you give me absolutely no credit at all?" he asked. I heard him walking circles around me. Or maybe I was spinning in circles. I couldn't be sure anymore. "Then again, you never were the brightest girl."

"I won't tell. I'll say that you kept me locked up in the dark. I'll say that I never knew. I will, honestly, I will!" I swore.

"Now, if honesty truly existed, would we even be in this situation? Just hold still, sweet girl, and it will all be over soon."

I felt the pair of hands grasp my shoulders once more, though I wasn't sure I could move anyway, and then I felt it. The cold metal of his knife ran down my neck. It hurt, oh God, it hurt like nothing I'd ever felt before. I felt my warm blood pouring out of the wounds, I could taste it bubbling in my mouth, out my nose. Tears streamed down my cheeks, and I prayed that it would end. I prayed for death. He laid me down and sat on my legs so that I couldn't fight. Don't be silly, I thought. *It was useless to hold me down. He didn't know I couldn't fight back, I wouldn't fight back. I was done.*

Then I heard Bailey once more. "Jaicey." She sounded fuzzy, or maybe that was just my blood-soaked thoughts, my ears pooled with blood. Her voice brought me back some focus. I knew I had to act fast if I wanted to save us. If I couldn't fight to save myself, I had to try and save her. I felt the icy blade dig into my neck once more, tracing designs into my skin, my skin on fire and raw with pain.

"Get off," I tried to scream, but I couldn't breathe through all the blood. As the blade dug into my neck once more, deeper than all of the other times, I was filled with adrenaline. I acted on impulse, jerking my arm free from the arms around my shoulders. I grabbed the knife from his hand, ignoring the blade as it dug into my broken, numb fingers. I stabbed the person holding me down from behind, digging it into his shoulders and dragging it toward me. He let go.

"Shit," he cursed loudly. "My shoulder! The bitch stabbed me!"

"Shut up, you idiot!" came Mr. Brown's voice.

I kicked and kicked until Mr. Brown fell off of my stomach and onto his side, spitting and cursing as well. I heard the knife clang to the ground, my fingers releasing it without warning. I felt around through the warm liquid to no avail. It was too dark and if I wanted to make it out alive, I couldn't stay in this room any longer, knife or no knife. I was free and I had to stay that way. I stayed down on my knees, keeping one hand pressed to my neck in an attempt to slow the bleeding. The pain was sharp, causing my eyes to water and my heartbeat to pound in my ears. I needed to get out of that room. I wanted to stay alive. Finally, I felt the door, freedom so close I could taste it. I tucked my hand under the bottom of the door and counted to three.

With one swift motion, the door swung open. I pushed myself up, my legs wobbly and weak underneath me, and then I bolted. I ran up a set of old wooden stairs, each one straining as I hit it. I ran as fast as my legs would carry me, my lungs burning for oxygen. Realizing I had no idea where I was and no idea how I was going to get out, I stopped. My whole body shook with pain and exhaustion. I gazed around the room, my vision blurring. The room I was standing in was old and dusty, basically empty. It was obvious that no one could have been living there. I ran through the room, beating on windows, searching for a door with no luck.

I spied a hallway out of the corner of my eye. Before I could make my way to it, I felt the knife dig into my leg, twisting its way up my thigh. I turned around, screaming as it tore through my muscles and nerves. I reached for the knife, feeling it tear me apart, and I just knew that I was dead. I fell to the ground, accepting defeat. It was over and I was going to die. He had won. He flipped me over, his glasses sliding off of his nose, his sweat dripping onto my face. He stared into my eyes with nothing but hatred.

"I was going to make this easy for you, but not now. No, you've asked for it now." He grabbed hold of my arms, slamming them down to my sides and holding the knife above me. With that simple move, I was given hope. Under my fingers, I felt something long and hard, a cool metal. I wrapped my fingers around it as the knife grew closer to my face. He leaned down, inches from my nose and I pulled the metal piece out,

slamming it into his head. He kneeled over, covering his head in pain and fell off of me once again. I looked at the thing in my hand. It must have been an old chair leg of some sort. I looked at him. He saw it coming.

The last time I saw Mr. Brown, his face showed only fear. Deep, immense fear. He screamed and I swung, showing no mercy. I hit him again and again until he fell silent. I grabbed the knife from where it had fallen in the floor, and I ran. I was almost to the door when I heard her soft scream. Bailey. I had almost forgotten her in my fear-filled state. I had to go back.

Without thinking twice, I turned around. "Bailey?" I called her name. "Where are you?" She didn't answer. I heard a door swing open. Someone was coming for me. I stepped over Mr. Brown's bleeding body without looking at him. I felt as though I were going to be sick again. I found the staircase quickly and forced my legs to go on as I ran back to the room where we had been kept. Everything in me hurt with each move, but I forced myself to go on. I swung open the door, feeling for a light switch, and flipped it on. The sight waiting for me was brutal. I bent over, emptying the feeble contents of my stomach onto the floor. Bailey had never left the room we were in. She had been there with me, tied up, the whole time. He had stabbed her over and over, her blood pouring out into the floor. Her pants hung loose around her ankles and her hair had been cut off.

I ran to her, dropping my weapons. "Oh, sweetie. Look what they did to you." I untied her carefully, noticing that her arm had been broken in several places. Her cheek had been slashed open, and her eyes were swollen shut. I pulled her pants up, feeling sick at how loosely they fit on her now. She couldn't walk, I knew. She couldn't even stand. Her legs shook under her weight and she immediately fell over, nearly smacking her head on the concrete. I wanted to cry at the hopelessness of it all.

No. *I told myself we were going to make it. I picked her up, using every bit of my strength to carry her out of that room. It must have taken me hours to get her up those stairs, but somehow we made it. Finally out of the house, I realized it was the middle of the night. I was thankful that there was no sun in the sky to burn my eyes. As I dragged her across the sand, I glanced back only once to look at the abandoned lighthouse where we were held captive.*

We'll never go back there, *I promised her mentally. My knees began buckling and I wasn't sure how much longer I could carry her, leaving our bloody trail as I went. I cried with relief as we reached Mr. Brown's car and I saw that he had left the keys still in it. I noticed another set of tire tracks in the muddy sand. Someone had left. They could be coming back. I pulled open the passenger's side door and lifted Bailey up into the seat, then stumbled my way to the opposite side. The world around me grew fuzzy and I wasn't sure I could even climb into the car, but I did. "We're going to make it, B. We're going to. You just hold on, okay?"*

I wasn't sure if she could hear me or if she was even still alive, and I was too afraid to check. I turned the keys in the ignition and began to drive. My hands were shaking as we pulled out, I had lost so much blood I could barely keep my eyes open. The adrenaline rush that had kept me going was wearing off by the minute. I just wanted to give up, to give in to sleep. I couldn't, I told myself, I wasn't going to let Bailey die. Not like this. It wasn't supposed to end like this. The clock on the dash said it was 4:04 in the morning. Somehow, I knew I would never forget that time.

I had always been an excellent driver, but sleep was causing me to swerve all over the road. I pulled out onto the highway, going around a big curve. I pressed my foot to the gas, I had to hurry. Bailey's blood soaked the seat she was in. Her bloody hand reached for mine. I heaved a sigh of relief, realizing she was alive. I locked my pinky with hers. We were going to be okay.

I watched the speedometer rise to 70 miles per hour, but that still wasn't fast enough. I was losing consciousness. I blinked, willing myself to stay awake. I pressed the pedal down harder, needing to go faster. Faster. It began getting harder to breathe, each breath more irregular than the last. Bailey was crying beside me. Her cries turned into soft screams as I watched her eyes glaze over. My best friend was dying before my eyes and I was falling asleep. There was nothing I could do. I turned on the air conditioner, wishing it would keep me awake.

My last thought was that we were going to be okay, that we had to be. I was very wrong.

I saw the headlights coming our way and I heard the horn blare. I felt the impact, heard the sickening crunch of metal on metal. Feeling my body catch fire was something I would never forget, smelling our flesh burning all around me and not being able to move.

My doctors said that with all the blood I had lost, it was a miracle I made it as far as I did. I passed out at some point, accepting death. I still had no idea where I was heading. The last thing I remembered, before waking up from my coma seven months later, was feeling Bailey's finger wrapped around mine. Even in the end, my best friend had wanted me to know that she was with me.

The police arrested Mr. Brown, who had survived my blows, but only barely.

I had thought that it was over. I had thought I could move on with my life, forget it had ever happened, but I had been so wrong. There had been someone else in the room that day. Someone I had forgotten about. Someone who had escaped through a door when I'd attacked Mr. Brown. It wasn't over, not yet.

CHAPTER TWENTY-EIGHT

"It was you," I said, looking up at Brayden with fearful disdain. "You were there when he kidnapped me. It was you that held me down while he tried to…while he stabbed me, stabbed Bailey. All along, all this time. It was you!"

"Yes, yes, Jaicey. It's about time you caught on." He took a step toward me.

I sat, frozen in ice-cold fear. "How could I have known? You never let me see your face. You left as soon as I knocked him out. You just left him there to die. You were a coward."

He lunged for me, grabbing a fistful of my hair and yanking me up to his face. "I knew that I had to leave in order to be able to come back for you. That was the goal, to finish what he started. You knew who he was. The police would be coming for him no matter what. But you hadn't seen me. You didn't know me. I was still free to carry out his plan. If you'd seen me, if I'd stuck around, I was just as doomed as he was. I couldn't let that happen.

He was counting on me." He tossed me down on the ground once more and I landed with a thud. He reached in the back pocket of his pants and pulled out a long, thin knife. This was just like my nightmare.

Had I somehow known all along? Had my subconscious been trying to tell me?

"But why?" I asked, desperately trying to buy time while I came up with a plan. I wasn't some scared, weak girl like I'd been last time. I could fight back now. "Why would you help him? Why would he do that? My parents gave him the money. He could've just let me go."

"He could never have let you go, Jaicey, don't you see? It was never about the money, never. I mean, yes, that was definitely the cherry on top of the whole thing, but it was always about you. About you and your spoiled rotten self and your rich mommy and daddy. You were just this girl who had the whole world handed to her. We had to show you how bad the world can be, don't you understand? It's so much darker than you believed. You had to understand that. We had to *help you* understand that. He said girls like you didn't deserve to keep living, carrying on every day with this perfect little life while the rest of the world suffers every day. You needed to know how it felt. You didn't deserve the life you were given. So, we took it from you."

"My life was not perfect," I spat at him.

He leaned down, smacking me hard across the cheek. "Don't lie to me."

"But why would you do this? I didn't even know you. What had I ever done to deserve this? He was my friend. I thought he was my friend, anyway. I cared about him."

"No, he wasn't your friend. He was your teacher. Girls like you don't know the difference. You think everyone loves you. You think everyone wants to help you out. Sorry, sweetie, but he hated you. He hated every single thing about you," he said through gritted teeth.

"Why? I want to know why. And you...you were kind to me. Why go through all the trouble to make me like you? You could've killed me so many times already, every time we've been alone. Why wait 'til now?"

"The waiting was his idea. He wanted to see you hurt even more. For what you did to him."

"Mr. Brown?" A chill ran down my spine. "You still talk to him? He still knows what you've been doing?"

"Of course he does. Dear old Dad knows everything."

"Dad?" I gulped. "He's your...*father?*"

"Come on, Jaicey, you aren't making this fun at all. I thought he told me you were smart. I figured surely you had that one figured out at least. Yes, he's my dad. After he beat the crap out of my mom one too many times, he was the only one I had left. We were a team, he and I. He taught me everything I know, raised me right."

I felt as if I were going to be sick. He twirled the knife around in his fingers, pressing it to each of his fingertips.

"The lighthouse...that was where he kept us, wasn't it? How could you take me there? Why would you take me there when you knew that's where he kept us? Why would you risk me noticing? I could've remembered everything right then, could've called the police."

He laughed, slapping his knees. "Are you kidding? I saw how you lied to everyone, including yourself, about what had happened to you. It was like nothing had ever happened, like that night never existed. I watched you for months, saw how you pushed your friends away as if you didn't know them. You don't think I noticed that all of the mirrors in your house were gone? That all the pictures stopped after that night? I asked you about Derek, and you pretended like he was just some guy. I saw you with your old friends; I saw how you acted like you didn't know them at all. He told me all about you, Jaicey. I knew everything about you. You could pretend that nothing had happened, that you'd never been the girl you were, but I knew better. The lighthouse was the final test. When you pretended not to recognize it, I knew I had you. You were so easy, just like he said you'd be. Didn't you learn your lesson not to trust people the first time?"

I was stupid—so stupid. I couldn't believe how idiotic I had let myself become. I reached up to my neck, tracing my fingers along each of the four scars he had given me.

"Did you really think that someone like me, someone normal, could love a scarred face like yours? Did you really think it could all be normal? That I hadn't noticed how deformed you are? Did you think I hadn't heard about you? The whole school knows what you did. They know it's your fault."

I pushed myself up from the ground, bolting from the room. I bounded into the kitchen, searching for the drawer with the knives. This was my only hope. I felt his hands grab my hair. I tensed up. He pulled me backward and stared into my eyes.

"It wasn't my fault," I muttered, trying to hold my head up to keep him from ripping my hair out.

"Of course it was. Who are you kidding?"

"It was your fault. *Yours.* I tried to save her." I sobbed, my eyes searching for his knife.

"You killed your best friend, Jaicey. You killed her, let her burn in that car after you fell out. You could have saved her." His cheek rubbed mine. He was so close, his face blood-red.

"No!" I screamed, hot tears pouring from my cheeks as years of heartache ripped through me hearing those words.

He pulled my head back, stepping out of the way and slamming my face into the counter. I bounced back, falling flat onto the kitchen tile. I rolled over, feeling for something to save me, anything to help. This time, there was nothing. This time, I wouldn't survive. Crying was all that I could do, and so I did it, loud and undaunted.

He stared at me from above. "You ready to die, Jaice? Do you want this to be over, once and for all?"

I nodded. I was ready. I just wanted it all to end. I thought for a moment about my parents. They'd come home and see my body, and I knew it would destroy them. I hoped he'd take me with him, that they'd never have to see me like this, never know how foolish I'd been. He leaned down close to my face again. I closed my eyes, waiting for the blow, waiting for the pain. Waiting.

"So now, let's finish this." He kissed me forcefully, shoving his whole mouth onto mine until I tasted blood. I wasn't sure if it was his or mine. I didn't fight back. There was no point. He pulled back, wiping blood from his mouth and smiling at me. I spit the blood from my tongue. "I love you, baby!" he screamed the phrase that had once made my heart ache with happiness and slapped me across the face. I grabbed my cheek, feeling more helpless than ever. My lips bled from being slammed onto the counter, and it felt like my front tooth had come loose. My head began to grow heavy, and the room felt dizzy. He hit me again and I felt my head slam onto the ground. It didn't even hurt.

This must be what dying feels like, I thought to myself, quiet and painless. I couldn't see him anymore, couldn't hear him, couldn't feel the blows I knew he was inflicting.

Suddenly, I heard a noise in the distance. I tried hard to pull my focus back, but it was no use. I heard glass breaking, wood cracking. I heard a voice, and then another. *Mumbling, mumbling. Footsteps.* My vision was so fuzzy. I wanted so badly to ask what was happening, why the room was going dark, why everything in me went numb. Instead, I was silent, staring at the flashing blue and red lights on my wall until everything went black. And then I was gone.

CHAPTER TWENTY-NINE

Someone was touching my face carefully with a cool hand. I could hear soft whispers but I wasn't sure who it could be. Gently, my eyes were pulled opened and a bright light was shone into them, back and forth between each eye. I wanted to tell them to stop but I couldn't find my voice. It was down in my stomach somewhere, I was sure. Hiding away.

The whisper grew louder, a soft voice. *Paisley*, it was saying. No. I tried to focus. *Lacey.* That wasn't it either. *Take me.* No, wait, I recognized the word then. *Jaicey.* My name. They were saying my name. The fuzziness began to clear from my vision and shapes started to form. I blinked. Once. Twice. There was my name again. *Jaicey? In you near me?* No, I tried to focus more, willing my eyes to see. *Can you hear me?* the voice asked. The blob in front of me began to take shape. *Mom.* The word formed in my head at seeing her face. *Mom.*

"Mom?" I croaked.

I stared up at her, tears on her cheeks, her face pale.

"Oh, sweetheart. Chuck! She's awake! She's awake!" She leaned down, sobbing into my chest.

I lifted my wrist up to pat her head but stopped when I noticed how heavy it was, a red cast around it. I saw my dad standing above me then, rubbing my mom's back. "How do you feel? Are you in pain?"

"No," I said, though that was a lie.

My mom sat up, staring at me. "We didn't know if you were going to make it. Oh, Jaicey, we should have been there. We thought it would be like last time...we were so worried we'd lose you again. I'm so sorry." She cried loudly. I didn't think I'd ever seen my mom cry before, not like this. "I'm just so glad you're okay. We were so worried." She kissed my head gently, her wet tears falling onto my skin.

"What happened?" I asked.

"Sweetheart," my dad said softly, "you were attacked. Do you remember that?"

Just then, a nurse rushed into the room, followed by a woman in a white coat and another in a dark suit. "See," the nurse said happily.

The woman in a white coat, the doctor, approached me. "Jaicey?"

I nodded.

"Can you speak?"

"Yes."

"Very good. Do you know where you are?"

She held her flashlight into my eyes, holding my eyelids open just as the nurse had done. "The hospital," I answered her. I hadn't forgotten this time. I wouldn't forget again.

"Very good. Are you hurting?"

I shook my head, but then answered honestly instead, "Well…a little."

"That's to be expected. We can give you something for the pain, but you've got a lot of healing to do."

I nodded.

"Can you tell me how many fingers you see?" She held up her hand.

Three. "Three," I answered.

"How is your vision? Everything clear?" She put her flashlight back into her pocket.

I looked around the room, checking for dark spots. "I can see," I answered.

"Good. Very good, Jaicey." She turned to my parents. "Everything looks good right now. Her pupils are responsive, and her CT checked out fine. If you experience anything weird," she looked at me with a serious stare, "anything at all, you let me know. Otherwise, just get some rest tonight. I'll check back with you in the morning."

I nodded.

"You are one lucky, lucky girl." She smiled at me, touching my arm lightly. As she walked out of the room, she said something to the nurse, who then approached me and stuck a needle into my IV. Relief was almost instant. I smiled gratefully to her as she walked out of the room as well.

Only the lady in the suit remained. "Hello, Jenny, Chuck. How are you feeling, Jaicey?"

My parents looked apprehensive. "I've been better." I

smiled at her. She looked familiar, though I wasn't sure why.

"Do you remember me?" I shook my head honestly. "That's perfectly okay." Her smile was friendly. "My name is Dr. Townsend. We met a few years ago after your first attack. I know you're having trouble remembering what happened. Do you know what I'm talking about right now?"

I looked at my parents and then back to her and nodded. "Yes, I remember."

"Good. You remember the man who attacked you two years ago?" I looked at my parents again.

Dr. Townsend spoke up. "Would you guys mind giving Jaicey and me just a few minutes?"

My parents looked back toward me. My mom frowned. "I don't know that that's the best idea. I mean, can't it wait? Jaicey needs us right now."

"I just need a few moments alone with her. You guys can wait right out in the hall, if that's okay with Jaicey?"

"What do you think, Jaice?" Dad asked.

I nodded. "I'll be okay."

They nodded, holding hands and walking out of the room, casting worried glances back my way. As the door shut, Dr. Townsend approached my bed. "Do you remember the man who attacked you two years ago?" she asked again.

"Mr. Brown." I nodded.

"Do you remember the man who attacked you tonight?"

I sucked in a painful breath. "Yes."

"I need you to say his name, Jaicey."

"Brayden."

"Thank you. Now, I need to ask you what happened tonight. Everything. It's important that we go over every detail."

I told her, closing my eyes and remembering each detail. When it was over, I opened my eyes, wishing I could forget. I covered my face in embarrassment. She stared at me. "What are you doing?"

I shook my head.

"Jaicey? What are you doing?"

I shook my head again. "It all just hurts so much."

"What hurts, Jaicey?"

"Everything. Everything that has happened. Remembering it all. It's like it never goes away. When I close my eyes, he's there."

She nodded, seeming to understand in a way I couldn't possibly expect her to. "I know it's hard, Jaicey, but you have to know that you're safe now. You're finally safe. The police will be here later to take your statement. Brayden is locked up. He's never going to be able to hurt you ever again. Do you understand?"

I nodded.

"But, Jaicey, I'm about to ask you to do something for me that isn't fair for me to ask. You have to remember what he did to you. You have to remember what you've been through."

I stared at her, eyes wide with shock.

"I know that sounds crazy, okay, but you have to. When people are faced with horrible, traumatic things, sometimes their brain's way of defending itself is to forget, okay? The problem is that you never actually

167

forget. Your brain just locks the memory away and it still haunts you. You're never able to deal with anything or to move on. Your parents said that you had forgotten your friends? Do you remember them now?"

"Yes."

"Good. That is what matters. Despite everything they've put you through, they couldn't take your friends or your family away from you. You've still got everything and everyone that matters. They, the monsters who did this to you, won't have anything ever again."

"I've still got everything?" I asked her, sudden anger boiling in my belly. "Did you really just say that? I've still got everything. Let me tell you what I still have: fear. Every time I close my eyes, there he is. When there's silence, I hear his voice. My skin is still crawling from his touch. He left me fear, and rage, and self-loathing. I don't have everything. He stole everything from me, do you hear me? Everything. I will never be who I was before him. I will never be able to forget. I'll never move on. Everything he did to me, everything he's done; I wear the proof on my neck, on my leg. I have nothing. I am nothing." Everything in me hated her. How dare she say that to me? How dare she act like she knew how I felt—how I *should* feel?

She spoke after a while, letting me cool down first. "Is that really how you feel?"

"Everything I've ever known is a lie. Now, out of nowhere, I remember what happened. What am I supposed to do with that? Where am I supposed to go from here?"

"Wherever you want." She smiled. "Jaicey, you go

wherever you want. You do whatever you want. Isn't that the point? Yes, you've got a long road ahead of you. Yes, it's going to be hard. Yes, it's going to hurt. Yes, you're going to have setbacks and bad days, but the point is that you get to do anything. You get to be anyone. Aaron and Brayden Brown will never have that chance. Never. Their lives are over, Jaicey. You get the chance to build yours up again."

I thought about her words, tossing them around inside my head.

"I'd like to ask you for another favor, if that's okay?" she asked.

"Okay."

"Would you come see me? I was thinking once a week, just to talk. No pressure. I want to make sure that we don't digress back into old habits."

I raised my eyebrows doubtfully. "For how long?"

"For however long you'd like. I tried to convince your parents that it was the right thing last time, but they insisted that you weren't ready. You'll be an adult soon, so it's your decision now. I really think it could help you, but ultimately it's up to you."

"My parents didn't want me to talk to you?"

"No." She shook her head. "After the first incident, you had significant memory loss. I told them that it was normal after such a severe trauma and that I thought, with time, it would come back. They didn't want to push you."

I nodded. "Can I have some time to think about it?"

She smiled. "Of course." She stood, walking to the door. "I'm going to let your parents back in now, okay?"

"Okay."

"If you need anything, anything at all, you call me."

"I will."

"Oh, and Jaicey?" she asked.

"Yeah?"

"I'm really glad that you're okay."

I smiled at her through the soreness of my face, trying to say thank you. She smiled back, opening the door. My parents flooded into the room. "Is she all right?"

"I'm fine, Mom," I answered, attempting to sit up.

"Don't sit up, sweetheart, not just yet. You'll hurt yourself."

I lay back down. They came over, both sitting on either side of me. Mom rubbed my scalp, where I could feel gauze taped to my skin. "You poor thing."

"You guys knew all along?" I asked, tears welling to my eyes. "How could you keep it from me, Mom? How could you let me believe that nothing had happened?"

Dad rubbed my arm. "We had no choice, Jaicey."

"What is that supposed to mean?"

"Honey," my mom whispered. "Listen, after what happened, you have to understand. We thought that we had lost you. You were in a coma for months, with doctors telling us there was a good chance you'd never wake up. A good chance that we'd never see you again. So, seven months later, when you woke up, it was like a miracle. You'd come back to us after all. But, Jaicey, you weren't the same. You were angry. You'd forgotten things, people...you were diagnosed with PTSD. Do you know what that is?"

I did. "Yes."

"Honey, you couldn't remember anything. You couldn't tell us what had happened. You didn't recognize your friends or Derek. It was like you'd just forgotten who you were. The police were able to arrest your teacher by running the plates on the car you'd been driving. Apparently, he'd owned some property near the lake, where they found him. They never told us where. We didn't ask. Your doctor told us that you would regain your memory after time, or at least that's what she believed. We started out taking you to sessions with Dr. Townsend, trying to get you to remember, but the sessions just upset you. We only cared that the man who had done this to you was locked up, and he was. We didn't see a point in putting you through those sessions just to have you remember something that would only hurt you. After a few weeks, we decided it was best to keep you home with us. To let you heal, to let you remember in your own time, on your own terms, Jaicey. We were only doing what we thought was best for you. We love you so much. We just wanted to keep you safe and happy, no matter what the cost."

"Jaice," my dad said, speaking up, "we didn't want to lie to you. Not once. That was never the intention. We just wanted to keep you safe. The less you remembered, the less painful we believed your life would be. We wanted to spare you any sort of pain we could."

"If we'd have just known, if we'd have just asked. He took you to the lighthouse, Brayden—that was where your teacher had kept you, wasn't it?" She said 'your teacher' as if it were taboo.

I nodded cautiously.

"Oh God." My mother cried out, looking at my father. "We could have stopped this. We could have saved you."

I squeezed her fingers with my good hand. "It's okay, Mom. It's over. It's all over."

She rubbed a piece of hair out of my eye, attempting to smile.

"What happened?" I asked.

Mom and Dad looked at each other, fear in their eyes, "What do you mean, sweetheart?"

"I mean, how did I get out? Did you all come home? I didn't fight back. I couldn't do it anymore." The question had haunted me since I'd regained consciousness, and now I needed to know.

"Oh." Dad frowned, sad tears in his eyes. "No, Jaicey. We didn't come home. We were still here when you arrived. We watched them wheel you past us. We didn't even know what had happened."

"But then, I don't understand. How can that be? How am I here right now? How am I alive?"

My mom looked up to my dad, who smiled at me. "Actually, on that note, I don't think we're the right people to answer that. You have a few visitors that we'd like to let in, if that's okay?"

I nodded, staring at the door as my dad approached it and pulled it open dramatically. He disappeared for a few seconds as we sat in silence, and reappeared with Mallory and Derek by his side. I gasped.

Mallory had tears streaming down her painted up face. Her hair had fallen from its formal style. She rushed toward me, her face red from crying.

"Jaicey!" she called as she ran into the room, holding

her arms out and falling onto my chest in sobs. Her touch hurt me, but I couldn't bear to pull away. She squeezed my shoulders, her whole body shaking. "Oh God, Jaicey. We were so worried about you. Oh God, oh God." She stood up, wiping her tears away and looking at me. "How are you?" She turned to my mom before I could answer. "How is she? What did the doctors say? Is she going to be all right?" And then back to me. "Are you going to be all right?"

"Yes," my mom and I answered in unison.

"She's going to be fine," my mom told her.

"Thanks to you." My dad spoke up, patting Mallory on the shoulder.

My jaw dropped. "You? Mal, it was you? You saved me?"

She smiled, her face beautiful even through her tear-stained makeup. "Not me. Derek. I called nine-one-one, but he saved you, Jaice. It was all him."

I looked up to Derek, who had been standing back near the door, still looking unsure. "You?"

He took a step forward apprehensively, then stopped. He cleared his throat. I noticed his eyes were swollen and bloodshot and he had a new cut on his lip. "Yeah, it was no big deal."

"No big deal?" Mallory turned to him. "Tell her what you did! Tell her, Derek."

He stood firm, though he looked unsure of himself. "I'm just so glad you are okay."

"Jaicey, he saved your life! We pulled up to your house tonight and heard screams. Derek looked in your window. He saw what was happening to you." Tears began to pour down her cheeks even though she was smiling. "He ran back to our limo and told me to call nine-one-one. Without even waiting for the police, he burst in the door and knocked him out. Just like that. He just pummeled him. It was like a movie or something. I couldn't even believe it."

"It wasn't like that," Derek said, his face turning red.

"Yes it was. Of course it was. Oh, Jaice, it was so heroic. He broke in your window and I heard his screams. Brayden, of course, not Derek. And then, Tyler and Alex came in and helped him tie him down until the police got there. It was just the most exciting thing. He was just amazing, Jaicey. So amazing. We all went into action. We found you on the floor. The police showed up. It was the scariest thing that's ever happened. Oh, I'm just so glad that you're okay." She smiled at Derek dotingly.

"Enough, Mallory. She's tired. She doesn't need to hear all of this." Derek shifted awkwardly by the bed.

Mom sat with tears in her eyes, confirming the story. My dad patted Derek on the back, not saying a word. Derek stood in the background, refusing to make eye contact with me.

"Mom? Dad?" I asked. "Mal? Could I have a second alone?"

"Of course," they all agreed happily, each patting me on the head as they made their way toward the door. Mom kissed my forehead. I watched Derek grab a hold of the door handle. "Wait," I called out to him.

They all turned back to me. "Stay." I stared at Derek, seeing him finally look me in the eye for the first time all evening. "Please."

He nodded, graciously stepping back and letting each of the others leave the room. He lingered by the door once it was shut.

"Is that true? What she said? That you saved me? That you broke into my house and attacked Brayden?"

"Well, it didn't happen like she said."

"How did it happen, then?" I asked him softly, watching him pace around the room, staying far from my bed.

"It wasn't heroic, Jaice. I mean, he punched me as often as I punched him. I was just lucky I caught him by surprise quick enough to knock the knife from his hand. If Tyler and Alex hadn't been there, I don't even know if I would've gotten him down. The police were there just as soon as we were trying to tie him up. It wasn't some heroic effort. We were just dumb kids getting in the cops' way."

"You broke into my house?"

"Yes, but it wasn't—"

I interrupted him. "You took on Brayden when he had a knife?"

"I knocked the knife away. I didn't even see it until I was already in the house. It was stupid, I know. I could just hear you screaming and I wasn't thinking." He looked at me seriously then.

"You attacked him? You knocked him out?"

"I hit him, yes, and he hit me right back." He pointed to the cut on his lip. "I was only able to take him down with Alex and Tyler's help. The cops said I should have waited for them. It was stupid, I know."

"I would've been dead," I whispered, hating the way it sounded out loud.

"What?" he asked, taking a step closer.

"I would have been dead, Derek. I would have been dead if you'd waited. You saved my life."

"No," he whispered, tears forming in his eyes. "No. No, I didn't."

"You did." I nodded. "You saved me."

"I did?" he asked, as a single tear rolled down his cheek.

"Why? Why would you do that?"

"You honestly have to ask?" He smiled, taking another step toward my bed.

"You love me?" I asked, my voice cracking.

He nodded, unable to speak.

"And I love you?" I asked again, feeling the tears begin to fall.

He nodded again. "Yes, Jaicey. Yes, we love each other very much. I've always loved you. Since you were six years old, running around covered in dirt in my back yard." He walked to my bed, holding his hand out. We stared at each other as minutes, hours, and years passed by, each of us speechless, tears flowing freely. He held out his hand, ready to touch my face, but stopped. "Is this okay?" he asked, wanting permission to touch me.

"Yes," I said, closing my eyes as his hand made contact with my cheek. His hand was warm and soft, familiar. He leaned down to sit on my bed, careful not to obstruct any wires or IVs.

"Do you remember everything?"

I opened my eyes. "Everything."

"You remember me? You remember us?"

"Especially you. Especially us."

He leaned into me, his face growing closer. I watched his lips parting, his eyes locking with my mine. Our mouths touched in slow motion, familiar and yet new all at once. Our kiss was amazing and beautiful, full of love and forgiveness and understanding. He moved his hand to my head, running his fingers slowly through my hair. He pulled back from our kiss before I was ready for it to end, my heart dancing in my chest. He kissed my cheek, where I knew a bruise must be; my nose where it was swollen and sore; and then, he stared at my neck. I didn't flinch as he ran his lips along every single scar, kissing each as he went.

I flashed back to Brayden, him telling me he could never love a scarred, ugly face like mine, then stared at Derek, more handsome and breathtaking than Brayden could ever be. "Are you sure about this, Derek?" I asked. "I'm not like I used to be. I'm scarred, for lack of a better word, and I don't just mean here." I touched my neck.

He stared at me, love filling his eyes, his head cocked to the side as if I were being ridiculous. He kissed me again, this time more quickly, but it still took my breath away. "Are you kidding? I've always been sure about us, Jaicey. You're beautiful. You're the most amazing girl I know. I love you."

I kissed him back then, wrapping my arms around his neck. The passion that filled our kiss had us both breathless and I felt our tears running down each other's cheeks, meeting and joining. As our kiss ended, he laid his head on my chest. "I've missed you." He sighed nervously.

"Derek?" I asked, suddenly realizing something.

"Yeah?" He sat up and looked at me.

"There's still something I'm confused about."

He held my hand. "What is it, Jaice? Ask me anything."

"How did you know to come? Why were you at my house? How did you know I was in danger?"

He smiled at me, kissing my nose. "I didn't, actually. It turned out to be good luck. I was just coming to get you to go to prom."

"What?" I asked, in between his kisses. "How can that be? I told you I was going to prom with Brayden."

"I know that." He kissed me again.

I put my hands to his chest, stopping his kisses momentarily. "I told you that I wouldn't go with you."

"I know that too." He smirked.

"So, then, why were you there?"

"I told you," he insisted. "I was coming to pick you up for prom."

I stared at him, my eyebrows raised, desperately trying to understand.

"Jaicey Paige Thomas, we have been talking about going to senior prom together since we were old enough to know what a prom was. We said we were going to show our grandchildren our prom pictures and tell them about how strong our love was, how it got us through everything." He took my hand from his chest and kissed it. "Did you really think there was any way in hell that I was going to let you go to prom with anyone but me?"

I smiled at him, overwhelmed with how good loving him felt.

"Besides," he threw in, "I knew you'd have to change

your mind once you saw how dashing I looked in my tux." He adjusted his collar cockily and grinned at me. Oh, how I'd missed that grin.

"Hey." I leaned up and kissed him. "I guess you're right. I'm so sorry you missed it, and Mallory, too. Where are the others? You said Tyler and Alex were with you all?"

"They're all out in the waiting room."

"All of you? Mal and Tyler and Alex and Alyssa?"

"Yes." He smiled. "And they're all going to be mad if I keep keeping you all to myself. Not that I don't enjoy it."

I covered my mouth, trying to push him away. "Oh, no. I didn't want you all to miss prom. What time is it? Did you already miss it? You can't miss prom just because of me. You have to leave, go. Enjoy the night."

"Shhh." He squeezed my hand gently. "Jaice, it's four in the morning. Prom is over."

"Oh no." I closed my eyes, covering my face with my hands. I felt awful. This wasn't how it was supposed to be. "I ruined this night for all of you."

"No." He pulled my hands down. "*No.* He ruined it for everyone, Jaicey, not you. We're all here because we want to be here. We wanted to stay with you and make sure that you were going to be okay. We're your friends, Jaicey, and we've missed you. God, we've all missed you so much. We weren't leaving here without you, and we weren't going to prom unless we were all together. We agreed."

"Really?"

"Really." He smiled.

"Can I see them?" I asked.

"Well, you'd better. They're all dying to see you. In fact,

I don't think they were going to give you a choice after a while." He stood.

"Wait, Derek."

"Yeah?" He stopped.

"Can I clean myself up a bit?" I asked.

"Babe, you look fine."

I cringed, realizing I could feel my blood drying on my face. "Please?"

"All right." He gave in. "Hang on a second." He pressed the button on my bed, and within seconds, a nurse was at my door.

"Is everything all right?" she asked, looking frazzled.

I smiled sheepishly. "I want to wash my face. Can I do that?"

She frowned. "I don't know. You aren't really supposed to be up."

"We can help her," Derek offered. "At least let her get some of the blood off of her face."

The nurse stared at me for a moment. "I guess I could clean you off."

"No." I shook my head. "I want to do it. I need to do it."

"Okay," she agreed finally. "But slowly." She walked to my bed, wrapping my arm around her neck. Derek walked to my other side, mimicking her actions. Together, they carried me to the bathroom.

"You don't feel dizzy, do you? Does your head hurt?" the nurse asked, watching me.

"I'm fine." I shook my head. Derek pulled the door open and ushered me in to the small bathroom.

"Can you hold her?" the nurse asked. "I'll get a washcloth."

Derek nodded, taking my weight in his arms. I looked up. We were standing in front of a mirror. Instinct made me close my eyes.

"Are you okay?" he asked, his lips on my ear.

I forced my eyes open slowly, staring at the mirror in front of me. I took a deep breath. Half of my head had been shaved, and I saw stitches running along my scalp. Nearly every inch of my face was bruised and swollen. My lips were bright purple, with dried blood in the corners. The silver of my eyes shone even behind my black and blue eyelids. I looked over my casted arm and my gauzed shoulder, and finally I allowed myself to look at my neck. Four thin, silvery lines ran down the right side, from my collar bone to just under my neck. The shadow of my hair almost hid them. I stared at myself, not believing that this was what I had made all the fuss about. These were the scars I had thrown my life away for. These were the scars he'd called ugly. They weren't ugly at all. They reminded me of my strength, my survival. They reminded me that I had made it, that I would be just fine. In fact, I realized then, I kind of liked them.

"Jaice?" he asked again, still waiting for my response. "Are you okay?"

"Yeah." I smiled at him in the mirror. "I'm going to be just fine."

CHAPTER THIRTY

After a ten day hospital stay, I was finally ready to go home. Mom and Dad were pacing around the room nervously as the doctor checked me over one last time. She wrote something down on my chart.

"You're absolutely sure she's okay?" my mom asked. "You're feeling okay, sweetheart?"

Dr. Hartwell smiled at my parents and closed the chart. "Mr. and Mrs. Thomas, Jaicey is doing wonderful. Her stitches are healing, and her scans are coming back perfectly. Overall, she is healing exceptionally well. She's ready to go home," she assured my parents. "She's going to be just fine."

My parents nodded, my mom clasping her hands together in front of her face. "Thank you so much, Doctor. You have been so wonderful."

"I'll need to see you back in six weeks to see how those stitches look and to remove your cast, but other than that, Jaicey, you're free to go."

"Thank you," I told her, already sliding off of my bed.

She turned off a machine beside me, smiled once more, and left the room. I started to follow her.

"Jaicey, wait," my mom called from behind me.

I turned around. "What's wrong?"

My dad took my mom's hand in his. "Honey, there's something we wanted to tell you. We wanted to wait until the right time. Until you were healthy."

"Okay?" I asked, and then, judging the look on Dad's face carefully, I sat down on the bed, bracing myself. "Are you okay?"

"I'm fine," he assured me. "It's just, well, this really isn't going to be easy to say. After the accident, after you lost your memory, we couldn't tell you. When I got sick—"

"We wanted to tell you, sweetheart," Mom interjected. "There was just never a good time."

"Just tell me," I said in a breath.

"Well, first of all, we want you to know how unbelievably proud we are of you and how much we love you," she said, looking to my dad.

"Everything's going to be okay now, Jaicey. We know that. I think you know that, but there's just one more thing that you should know, if you're really ready to face everything."

"Please just tell me." If they didn't say it soon, I was going to explode. What in the world had them so flustered?

Dad looked at Mom, who looked at me with tears in her eyes; their hands were held together as if by glue. Dad took a deep breath. "Jaice, honey…Bailey's alive."

CHAPTER THIRTY-ONE

I walked out of my hospital room as if in a trance, both of my parents by my side. We formed a solid wall, ready to take on anything. We walked past the nurses' station and down a long hall. We stopped in front of an elevator and Dad pressed the button for the second floor. They'd been here before, he told me, so they didn't need to ask for directions. How many times had my parents visited my best friend without my knowledge?

We stepped into the elevator solemnly, each of us staring at our reflections in the door. We went down three floors before the signal above the door sounded. They glided open, and I stared at a gray wall with a sign that read **Long-Term Care**. We walked out the doors, down a hallway, and around a corner before we stopped at door 713. There was no sign to let us know that this was Bailey's room, nothing to separate her door from any of the others. She was just a room number.

"Are you sure about this?" Dad asked. "We can come back another time."

"No," I said firmly, hoping my voice sounded braver than I felt. "I have to see her." I put my hand to the knob, feeling the cool metal press into my hand, and willing myself not to get my hopes up. I'd heard what my parents said, and I knew what to expect. Holding my breath, I turned the knob. There she was. Her curly, black hair fell loosely around her face, her long, dark eyelashes peeking out from above her closed eyes. I watched her chest slowly rise and fall. She could have been sleeping.

I reminded myself that this was what I had known it would be like. A coma. Mom had told me everything. Bailey was in a coma, had been for nearly three years, and she wasn't coming out. I heard someone clear their throat in the corner of the room and looked up.

"Mrs. O'Malley," I cried out, seeing Bailey's mother sitting in the corner. She was smaller than the last time I'd seen her, her hair much more gray. She stood up, holding her arms out to me, pulling me into a hug.

"Jaicey," she cried. "Oh, sweetheart." She buried her face in my neck. I'd missed her hugs.

"It's so good to see you," I told her.

"It's good to see you, too." She smiled at me. Her eyes looked much older than they had three years ago. I could see how much she was hurting. "Bailey would be glad that you got to come see her, too."

I looked back to the bed where my best friend lay. "Could I sit by her?"

"Of course." She stepped back, smiling lovingly at her daughter.

I approached the bed, looking her over. I took hold of her hand, rubbing my thumb over her fingers. It broke my heart to see that her usually painted nails were now dull and plain. I saw the burn scars on her face, running down her arms and chest, though she still looked as beautiful as ever to me. I leaned onto her bed, trying to be careful.

"You won't hurt her, Jaice," her mother told me.

Upon her word, I pulled myself up onto the bed, crossing my legs. I smiled down at her, rubbing my hands through her hair. "She won't wake up?" I asked, though I knew the answer.

"No." Her mother shook her head.

"Is it—" I stopped myself, trying not to cry. "Is it my fault? The accident? Is that what caused it? Did I do this?" I felt the all-too-familiar tears returning again.

"No, sweetheart." Her mom shook her head. "No. You didn't do this. You were the best friend she could've ever asked for, and I'm thankful every day that she had you, and that she had you with her in the end. You'll never know what that means to me." She approached me, rubbing my back. My parents stood near the bed in complete silence.

I couldn't stand all of the crying. It was making me sick, but I just couldn't stop. "Is she in pain?"

"No," her mom answered again. "She's not in any pain. She doesn't feel anything anymore. She's at peace."

I nodded, staring at her burns. "Where is Mr. O'Malley?" I asked, the question out of my mouth before I even realized it. Had that been rude?

"Oh." Her mom covered her mouth. "It's just too hard on him, honey. After the accident we were both here every day for a year. We waited by her bed, praying, just praying that God would send our little girl back to us. We've accepted that she's not coming back, Jaicey."

"But how?" I asked through my tears.

She walked closer and smiled at me through tear-filled eyes. "Our baby girl is gone, and we will never ever be okay with that, but we also know that our little girl no longer feels any pain. We take comfort in knowing that she is gone, in knowing that she was saved from having to suffer anymore than she did. We know that she is in a better place and that she'll never have to deal with the awful things that man did to her. She'll never have to feel pain or fear or worry ever, ever again. Our daughter is at peace, Jaicey, Bailey is at peace and we are finally ready to make peace with that."

"What does that mean?" I asked, allowing her to hold me in her arms and rock me.

"You know," she told me, "I always thought of you as a daughter. I mean, you and Bailey were practically sisters, so you may as well have been my daughter, too."

I nodded, not moving from her arms, my tears soaking her shirt.

"George and I have had three years to grieve for Bailey. We've had three years to accept what happened, but we have the rest of our lives to remember her, to celebrate her life. She doesn't have to be here for that. She's in here." She patted my chest, pointing to my heart. "We don't need her body to stay with us to remember her."

"You're saying you're going to let her die?" I asked, pulling away from her. "You're going to just let her go?"

She shook her head. "She's already gone. She's been gone."

"So, why bring me here?" I looked to my parents. "You knew about this? You just wanted me to feel losing her all over again? How could you do this?"

"Jaicey, sweetheart," my dad said. My mom was choking back tears.

Mrs. O'Malley held up her hand. "I asked them to bring you. Ever since the accident, your parents have been so kind, helping us with the medical bills. Keeping her in a place like this has been taxing on our family, but we just needed to keep her here. We needed her with us. Four months ago, we decided that it was time to let her go, but we couldn't do that without talking to you. Bailey was just as much your family as she was ours, and it just didn't sit right with us to leave you out of the decision. So, Jaicey, I'm asking you, can you help us let our baby go? Can we let B go home?"

I shook with sobs, staring at her. I felt hands on all sides of me, rubbing my back in an attempt to comfort me. I didn't know if I could ever feel comfort again.

"I know it isn't fair." She sobbed. "We've had years to deal with this decision and I'm giving you just a few moments. Please understand that we don't have to do this if you aren't ready. We can keep her here for as long as you need."

I looked at my best friend, at how little she'd changed over the last three years, and then I looked at Mrs. O'Malley and just how *much* she'd changed. It obvious that Bailey wasn't the one suffering here; it was her family. I, too, would now be on that list. Could I stand to come here every day? To see her hooked up to machines keeping her alive? Would she want me here wasting away, waiting for her to wake up but knowing she never would? Or would she want me out living, remembering her, celebrating her? What about her family? What would I want her to do if the situation were reversed? I had thought, initially, that this would be enough. That having her body— feeling her heartbeat, and watching her breathe—would be enough. I knew now that I was terribly wrong. My best friend was gone and nothing was going to change that.

"You're right." I wiped my eyes.

Mrs. O'Malley looked at me. "You're sure?"

"I'm sure. It will never be okay, but whether or not we keep her body here, you are right. Bailey hasn't been here in a long time. We'll keep her with us every day, while we're out living. It's what Bailey would have wanted."

Her mom began sobbing again, hugging me tightly. "Thank you, you brave girl. Thank you," she cried.

"Can you do me one favor, though?"

"Anything." She nodded.

"Can you just give me one night with her?" I asked. "Just to say goodbye?"

She wiped her tears then, her face red. "Of course, I can."

"I'll need some red nail polish." I tried to laugh through my tears.

"We can get that," Mom said.

They, all three, kissed my head, leaving the room in tears. Mrs. O'Malley cast one last look at me as she shut the door, and I saw peace in her eyes. I knew I was making the right decision. I turned around so that I could lay next to Bailey in bed and kissed her forehead. I locked my pinky around hers.

"You'll be safe now," I promised her. I rubbed my fingers over the burns on her arms and hands, and then I cried with my best friend for the very last time.

EPILOGUE

TWENTY YEARS LATER

"They say that time takes everything, Jaicey, and in time, I think you'll find that it does. It takes away everything you need it to and everything you wish it wouldn't. Youth, heartache, loved ones, sadness, sanity, memory; you'll find nearly everything falls prey to time at some point or another. You'll often hear that time heals all wounds, and I believe that it does, but more importantly, I believe that time is cruel. It doesn't pick and choose. It doesn't care if you are a good person. In the end, it only cares that it keeps moving, keeps taking. What about the truth?"

I looked up at Dr. Townsend, her graying hair a prime example of all that time takes. "What about it?"

"Sometimes we try to pick and choose truth—our truth. I think you've learned the hard way that you can't decide your own truth. There's truth, Jaicey, and there's lie. I know this sounds absurd, but what you've told me over these past years, it all makes sense. Sometimes, and I've seen it time and time again, sometimes you lie to yourself without realizing that you are lying. It's a defense mechanism that the brain has picked up. In your case, you lied to yourself because you needed to; because you couldn't deal with the truth at that point in your life. Because you, mentally, weren't able to accept what had happened. If you lie to yourself long enough, sometimes it becomes real. You'd never have known any different if it weren't for Brayden. It's likely your memory of the incident would have stayed locked up forever."

I nodded, twisting the hem of a pillow between my fingers.

Dr. Townsend smiled. "So, you said that your mother died when you were fifteen because, in your mind, she had. The mother that you had grown up with wasn't who was sitting across from you at the table anymore. You said you didn't want to drive because you thought that you had killed your best friend while driving. It was easier for you to pretend you had never been popular than to remember a time when you were. As messed up as you believe this all was, I promise you I've seen worse."

We were silent for a moment.

"I'm glad that I could convince you to come. I know this anniversary is a hard one for you and I like to think that it helps you to be able to be here, to talk through it again. Your journey amazes me." She leaned across the table. "So, that being said, I'm going to leave you for exactly one hour. I want you to write down all that you can for me about what you remember."

"Is this really necessary? Every year? I'm not going to forget."

She pressed her lips together. "I don't want this to be a chore. I like to make sure that your memory isn't slipping, that you aren't degenerating back to the memory loss, but this isn't mandatory, no."

"But you think it helps me? It keeps me from forgetting?"

"I think so, yes."

"Okay," I agreed, taking a pen and notepad from her.

"One hour," she reminded me. "Don't think of it as a test. Just tell me your story. Your time starts now. Good luck." She looked at her watch as she walked out of her office. I flopped back onto the couch, placing the notebook on my knees and beginning to write.

WHEN THE HOUR was up and she returned, I had written way more that I had actually planned. She took the notebook happily. "This is more than usual." She read silently, her eyes locked on the pages as they turned. When she finally finished, she closed the notebook and looked up. "This is exactly what I've been looking for. This is quite a breakthrough, Jaicey. Could I ask you a favor?" She held the notebook tight to her chest.

"Sure," I told her.

"Would you mind if I read a bit of this tonight at my seminar? I really think it could help some of my other clients."

I nodded. "I guess I don't mind, but it isn't very good. I wasn't trying to make it perfect."

She placed her hand onto my shoulder. "I didn't want perfect. This is real. This is honest. I couldn't have asked for better."

I SHOWED up at the seminar that night a few minutes early, hoping to find a good seat. I sat in the crowd and listened to the different stories being read, stories of people's tragic and unfair lives. When it came time for Dr. Townsend to read mine, I held my breath. I felt Derek lace his fingers through mine, just as he had on graduation night, at our wedding, and as we had brought our beautiful little girl into the world. My father had been present for all three events. He squeezed my hand lovingly as she began reading aloud.

"Someone once told me that eventually time takes away everything you have—everyone you love, your dreams, your memories, your fears. It takes everything you've ever had, and you never notice until it's gone. The same person told me that though time is known to heal, time is actually cruel. Despite every single thing time steals from you, it will never take one thing away. No matter how many nights you spend awake, how many meals you miss, or how many stares you try not to notice; time is just time, and no matter how much time passes, it will never let you forget the truth."

BONUS CHAPTER

Author's Note:
This was a bonus chapter I had written that didn't make it into the novel, as I could never find a good place for it. But, I really love it and thought you all might enjoy it, too!

Jenny and Chuck Thomas were awakened by the phone ringing loudly throughout the house. Jenny sat up in bed instantly, dread filling her stomach. Who on earth would be calling this late?

"Chuck?" She patted her husband's stomach.

He stirred. "What is that?"

"The phone," she told him, leaping out of her bed. She rushed across the room, toward the dresser by her door.

"Hello?" she answered without looking at caller ID.

"Hello, is this Jennifer Thomas?" the voice on the line asked her. It was a man's voice, she could tell. It sounded muffled, strained even.

"Yes, hello? Hello? Who is this?" she asked, her senses heightening. Chuck sat up in bed, rubbing his eyes.

"We have your daughter, Mrs. Thomas. We have Jaicey."

"*You what?*" she screamed into the phone, her hands shaking. Her husband was at her side instantly.

"What's wrong? Who is it?"

Tears filled her eyes as she hit speaker phone, allowing her husband to hear what she could.

"We have your daughter. She's alive...for now. You need to get all the money you have together. We'll set up a meeting point for the drop off."

"Is this a kidnapping?" Jenny asked.

"Don't hurt her." Chuck told them, both of their eyes locked on each other's in cold fear.

"No police. You have twenty-four hours." *Click.*

The line went dead and Jenny froze.

"Was there a number on there? Where were they calling from?"

"Where is Jaicey supposed to be? Isn't she with Bailey? Can we call her mother?"

"How much money do we have in the account? Do you think this is a joke?"

"Should we try to call her? Have you talked to her today? Do we have Bailey's number if Mrs. O'Malley doesn't answer?

"What are we going to do, Chuck?"

"Where could she be?"

"How long has she been missing?"

Questions flowed out of them like lava as they bustled around the room, running circles with no sense of what they should be doing.

Jennifer picked up her phone again, her hands shaking.

She dialed Bailey's number from memory and listened to it ring.

"Hey, y'all, it's Bailey's phone. Sorry I missed you. Leave a message and maybe I'll call you back." She heard Bailey's laughter at the end of the message.

"Bailey, this is Jennifer Thomas. I need you to call me back right now."

She hung up the phone, staring at her husband. He nodded. "Call her mom."

She did as she was told, all of her own mental processing had suddenly quit working. The line rang several times before a groggy voice answered the phone.

"Mrs. O'Malley? Hey, it's Jen Thomas. Are the girls there with you?"

"Jen? What's wrong, honey? The girls are in Charleston with their friends, didn't Jaicey tell you? They'll be back tomorrow night."

"I need you to call and find out if that's where they are. *I need you to call right now,*" Jenny screamed at her.

"What's happening? Is everything all right?"

"I just got a ransom call." The words felt wrong coming out of her mouth. Cold chills ran down her arms.

"A ransom? Like a kidnapping?"

"I need you to tell me if the girls are safe…I need you to do it now."

The line went dead as the worried parents went into action. Chuck walked back into the room. "Derek? Have we tried Derek?"

Jenny shook her head, dialing the number. "Rebecca, it's Jen. Has Derek seen Jaicey?"

"What?" Her voice cracked as she spoke.

"Has Derek seen Jaicey today? Has he talked to her? Does he know where she is?"

She seemed to wake up at that point. "Jen, what's going on? Is Jaicey okay?"

"I don't know," Jenny admitted to her best friend. "I don't know what's happening."

Within hours, the Andersons and O'Malleys were all piled into the Thomas's living room.

"I don't understand how this could've happened," Tiffany O'Malley cried.

Derek sat in the recliner, his head in his hands. "I honestly don't know. We were at Dan Murphy's party. I didn't see them...we were supposed to leave together but I couldn't find them. We'd been fighting so I thought they left without me. I'm so sorry, Mrs. Thomas. I should've stayed and looked for them."

"They were never in Charleston?"

"Not that I know of," he replied.

"When is the last time you spoke to them, Derek?"

"At the party on Friday night."

"Have you tried to call her?"

"*It's been two days,*" Jenny shouted. "God knows what he could've done to them."

"Have you called the police?" Rebecca asked.

"No police!" Tiffany shouted. "They said no police, right? No police!"

Jenny nodded. "We can't call the police. We have to do whatever they ask. Anything."

Everyone nodded solemnly.

"We've pulled everything we have out of the account. It's all yours," Rebecca told Jenny.

"Us too," Tiffany told her. "Are you sure he didn't mention Bailey? They have to be together, right? She's not answering her phone. She always has her phone."

Jenny couldn't help but notice the look on Tiffany's face, telling her she hoped by some chance that Bailey wasn't with Jaicey. She hoped her daughter, at least, was safe. Jenny couldn't help but feel the same, evil way. Hoping that somehow it was a mistake, that they'd gotten the wrong girl...any other girl.

She stopped short as the phone rang. This time, she snapped it open immediately.

"Hello?" she called into it.

"I'm going to let you talk to your daughter. Just a second or two. And then we're going to discuss the ransom." This man sounded articulate, smart. How had he gotten caught up in a mess like this?

"We have your money. As much as you could want. We'll meet you, wire it, whatever you need. Please just don't hurt her," she pleaded into the phone, not able to focus as every eye in the room grew teary.

She heard the man mumbling something in the background, heard something swishing up against the speaker. She waited, praying to hear her daughter's voice.

And then, "Mom?"

ENJOYED THE MISSING PIECE?

Thank you so much for reading The Missing Piece! This book is so special to me because even though it was my third published book, it's actually the first novel I ever finished. I guess you could say this book started it all.

If you enjoyed Jaicey's story, I'd love to ask you for a small favor. Reviews are so important to us as authors. So many times, a reader's decision to try out a new book or author is influenced by reviews!

As an author who works so hard to bring the very best stories to my fans, I would really appreciate it if you'd consider leaving me a review. It doesn't have to be long, just a few words will do if you aren't sure what to say. A simple "I enjoyed it" or "This book changed my life, I'll be naming my firstborn Jaicey!" (LOL!) will do.

If you'd like to leave a review, please visit: https://amzn.to/2Z3HR8N

Thank you so much in advance!

XO,

Kiersten

ACKNOWLEDGMENTS

As always, I have so many people to thank for helping me to bring this book to life.

First and foremost, to my amazing husband and sweet baby girl, thank you for holding down the fort when I'm lost in my own world and for believing in me enough to let me chase this dream. I love you both and am so thankful you can handle my crazy!

To the rest of my family, thank you for your unending support and excitement with step of this process. You'll always be my original Fan Club! ;)

To my Twisted Readers, Street Team, and Review Team: thank you for all you do for me. Thank you for never stopping believing in me. Thank you for loving my characters like I do and for understanding me in a way no one else can. Our group is so full of love and support. *I see that.* As much as it's growing, it still feels like a family and that's all because of how amazing you are, not only to me, but to each other. (P.S. If you want to be a part of a community like that, we'd LOVE to have you. Just click here to join!)

To all the bloggers, fellow authors, and sweet readers who help spread the word about my stories every day just for the love of reading. I can't tell you enough how thankful I am to know you all. Thank you for believing that the written word can change your mood, your day, and ultimately, your life.

And, lastly, to you, if you're reading this. Whether you loved or hated this book, thank you for reading and for supporting art. I would be nowhere without readers like you and I am eternally grateful and humbled that you chose to spend your time and money on a world that once existed only inside my head.

If you're new to my books, I hope Jaicey's story will have you rushing to read more of my work. If you've been with me for a while, I hope this book was everything you've come to love about my work and nothing you expected all at once! Thank you for continuing to support me.

ABOUT THE AUTHOR

Kiersten Modglin is an Amazon Top 30 bestselling author of award-winning psychological suspense novels and a member of International Thriller Writers. Kiersten lives in Nashville, Tennessee with her husband, daughter, and their two Boston Terriers: Cedric and Georgie. She is best known for her unpredictable suspense and her readers have dubbed her 'The Queen of Twists.' A Netflix addict, Shonda Rhimes super-fan, psychology fanatic, and indoor enthusiast, Kiersten enjoys rainy days spent with her nose in a book.

Sign up for Kiersten's newsletter here:
http://eepurl.com/b3cNFP
Sign up for text alerts from Kiersten here:
www.kierstenmodglinauthor.com/textalerts.html

www.kierstenmodglinauthor.com

www.facebook.com/kierstenmodglinauthor
www.facebook.com/groups/kierstenstwistedreaders
www.twitter.com/kmodglinauthor
www.instagram.com/kierstenmodglinauthor
www.goodreads.com/kierstenmodglinauthor
www.bookbub.com/authors/kiersten-modglin
www.amazon.com/author/kierstenmodglin

ALSO BY KIERSTEN MODGLIN

The Reunion